BURNED

IVY JACKSON

Editing: Sandra at One Love Editing

Proofreading: Victoria at Cruel Ink Editing + Design

Formatting: Victoria at Cruel Ink Editing + Design

Cover Designer: Jillian Liota at Blue Moon Creative Studio

DEDICATION

For my aunt, who I got so many precious years with.

A NOTE ABOUT THE CONTENT OF BURNED

This book contains discussions about animal cruelty. While it is brief, it is discussed on page. Grief due to the loss of a loved one is present throughout.

Cystic Fibrosis is also discussed at length. It is a rare inherited disease that is life threatening, even with treatment.

If you would like to learn more about this disease, please visit the Cystic Fibrosis Foundation's website. My family's experience with this disease will be discussed in the acknowledgements.

A PLAYLIST TO GET YOU IN YOUR ✦ COWBOY ERA ✦

"Me On You" - Muscadine Bloodline

"She's Country" - Jason Aldean

"Honky Tonk Badonkadonk" - Trace Adkins

"Goodbye Earl" - The Chicks

"Tequila Makes Her Clothes Fall Off" - Joe Nichols

"Boot Scootin' Boogie" - Brooks & Dunn

"Flatliner" - Cole Swindell & Dierks Bentley

CHAPTER ONE

Poppy

I WILL NEVER FORGET my first sexual experience.

I had just turned sixteen — yes, I was a late bloomer — and the guy I had a crush on was picking me up in his purple, vintage Mustang. One from like the sixties or something because that thing didn't even have proper seat belts. And when I say *he* was picking me up, I mean he and *his mom* were picking me up. Because he still only had his permit and needed a licensed adult in the front seat.

So we get to his house, and his mom goes off somewhere and leaves us to hang out. His house was massive. I can't remember what his parents did, but they made fucking bank. He had the entire lower level that walked out into the woods all to himself. Which begs the question, why didn't we just stay in his room?

Who knows. He decides we need to take a ride on

the four-wheeler. And I'm ecstatic, right? Because anything that gets me closer to him is a win for me. I get to hold on while we traipse around in the woods, getting muddy and doing things we probably shouldn't.

But the next thing I know, we're parked in a clearing, and I'm *completely* naked and lying on the seat of the four-wheeler with my feet propped up on the back bars. It's like I was getting ready for a damn pap smear. Knees up and spread wide.

And he's standing next to me, his cock out while he strokes it, and his other arm extended straight while he finger bangs the absolute shit out of me. And I mean *bangs*. Dude does not hold back and at the same time has no fucking clue what he is doing. It's stiff and uncomfortable, and my sixteen-year-old self had no clue what to do with that.

Other than to fake it. And that's exactly what I did. I knew what it felt like to have an orgasm. I was a late bloomer with other people, not with myself. I wasn't a nun. So I faked it, making noises like the girls do in porn because I thought that's probably what men liked.

Anyway, I "finished" and then stumbled my way through the most awkward hand job in the history of the Earth, with him getting annoyed that I wasn't holding it right. But, Jesus Christ, it was the size of my forearm. I didn't have the knowledge of how to deal with any dick, let alone one *that* large.

But I managed, and he eventually finished. He

cleaned up on some leaves, and we both got dressed and went back to his house. I'm pretty sure he took me straight home after that, but honestly, I blocked everything out.

And that one experience set the tone for how all of my sexual encounters were going to go for the rest of my life. Because ever since then, I haven't had a single orgasm that I haven't given myself. I have mastered the art of faking it — squeeze the Kegels over and over again, moan *just* enough to make it believable, and act out of breath afterward when they eventually collapse from their own exhaustion.

That's what I'm hoping will happen right now. As Ethan's hips slap against my own, I send up a silent prayer that it will end as I squeeze my thighs and arch my back. The show is about to begin, and if I know him at all, it should make him race toward the finish line.

I don't even know why I bother. Honestly, I like my alone time, and I can please myself better than any of the men I've dated. But I'm not asexual. There have been times I've wondered, but I'm not. I know I'm not because even when I know that the guy probably isn't going to be able to get me off, I still get all the warm and fuzzy butterflies.

I still get wet. I still want them to touch me and try. And I really, really want it to happen. I want to meet the guy that's going to work my body just as well as I can.

Maybe one day, I'll meet a guy who can make my toes curl and my eyes roll back.

But for now, I'm stuck with Ethan. Well, for this one last time anyway. I've been kind-of-sort-of dating him for the past six months. We met at my weekend job at the dog boarding and daycare center, and he's funny and kind. So I gave it a go.

The show ends, and he collapses on top of me and kisses my temple before rolling off the side. I look over at him, watching his handsome face go all blissed-out while he comes down from the high. He has pretty natural blond hair that many women would kill for, and those eyes…don't get me started on his eyes. They start off light blue around the pupil and have a dark ring around the outset.

"You're sure you have to go?" he asks, turning his head to face me.

I blink out of my thoughts and take a deep breath, looking toward the ceiling.

"I do," I tell him, a smile pulling at the corners of my mouth. "My flight is booked, and they expect me first thing Monday."

He sighs, but I'm too busy being excited for my next adventure to worry about how he feels. I've been bouncing around my whole life, from moving all through high school, to twice in college, and then to San Francisco afterward. And in between all of that, I've never held down an actual job. I mean, I've had jobs.

I've worked at restaurants, and in retail, and most recently, as a nanny and a part-time dog day care attendant.

I got a degree in English language, and I really thought I would waltz out with that degree and right into a speech therapy job. It was what I always wanted to do — work with kids in school to get over stutters and other speech impediments so they'd feel more confident about themselves.

One thing led to another, and that job just kept slipping out of my grasp. So many wanted a master's degree, and I didn't have the money to go to school for a second time around. So I thought I would get some odd jobs here and there, and that would help me save up to go back.

But school is expensive, and so is existing. Between groceries, rent, and credit card bills, I wasn't able to save anything, let alone enough to go back to school. And the thought of applying for more student loans made me want to throw up. So I took the first, best-paying job I could find.

Being a nanny is great. I get to work with kids, and I get paid out the ass for it. Meanwhile, I get to live in their house, drive their spare car, and not pay any rent whatsoever. So for the past two years, I've been able to pay off all my credit card debt, make a dent in my school loans, and save up to move somewhere new. Somewhere I can start fresh. Again.

And when I stumbled upon this job on a ranch in Montana, I thought, holy shit, that sounds fun as hell. They're hiring someone to come on and help them with all of their rescue animals, and even though I only have experience with dogs, they were eager to have someone with any experience at all.

My mom thinks I'm insane, moving to the middle of nowhere, Montana, but I couldn't be more thrilled. I'm excited for the fresh mountain air and the change of scenery. The city is loud and constantly awake, but I want the sleepy pace of Cane Creek, Montana.

"You know," Ethan starts, rolling over to sit up on his elbow. "We could try to make the long-distance thing work. I could fly to you, you could fly to me. It's not that far away, and god knows you'll probably move on once the summer is done."

That's what I'm known for — never staying in one place for long. Never holding down a job, a relationship, or a place to live. Everyone has come to expect it of me, even Ethan. It stings, knowing that's what everyone thinks of me. Not that I haven't earned it — I have. But I still don't like it. I want to be seen as someone to be relied on, someone stable and...adult. I may only be twenty-six, but that's plenty old enough to be seen as a grown-up, for fuck's sake.

"No, Ethan," I say, rolling away from him and out of his bed. "I don't want anything long-distance. And I certainly don't want to bet against myself and this job already. Just because the trial period is only for the summer doesn't mean I won't choose to stay on permanently after."

"I'm sorry, I didn't mean—"

"No, it's fine." I hold up my hand, cutting him off but giving him a sympathetic smile as I get dressed. "Today was the last time, okay? You're great, but this is a fresh start for me. I want to finally start my life. And that means not bringing anything with me. Including you."

Without a second glance at him, I pick up my bag and leave his room. I rush down the steep stairs of his town house and out the front door into the misty fog that's rolling up from the bay. Closing the door behind me, it finally feels like I'm starting over.

Nothing holding me down. No strings. Nothing between me and the ranch in Montana. Smiling to myself, I walk toward the BART and say goodbye to this city.

CHAPTER TWO

Rhett

THE SMELL of coffee assaults my nose as I make my way into my parents' house. Momma gets up every morning and makes sure there's coffee ready to go for any of the guys who work on the ranch. Their home is the main hub for food and snacks, no matter how many times I tell her to stop letting these men take advantage of her kindness.

"Sun isn't even up yet," I say when I see my dad sitting at the kitchen table, reading the paper. His grey hair is almost white now, and his glasses sit low on his nose as he looks up at me, his brown eyes matching the color of my own.

"Habit," he tells me, setting the paper down on the old wooden table. It's been in the family since I was a little kid. We've had countless meals on it, and my sister used to sit there to do her breathing treatments every morning. I blink the memory of Addie away.

"Yeah?" I ask as I take a cup of coffee out of Momma's hands. They're fragile, with crooked fingers from the arthritis that cropped up early in her life. "Must be important if it gets you down here and dressed before 6:00 a.m., Pops."

Normally, he's walking around in baggy boxers and a loose T-shirt, not caring that men are running in and out of here like it's a soup kitchen. Guess he earned it after all those years of running the ranch.

"We hired a new ranch hand."

I set my mug down and press my palms into the cool granite of the countertop. I hang my head.

"We don't need a new ranch hand," I bite out. "Nor can we afford one."

"You've been running your brother ragged ever since Tommy left. That poor boy needs a helping hand with those rescues you insist on taking in."

I swallow the retort I want to say because he's right. I do insist on taking in these damn rescue animals, all for Addie. It was Addie's dream to run a rescue, and this is the only way I know how to honor my sister's life.

Cracking my neck, I turn around and face him. Momma takes a sip from her own mug and watches us with a little smile on her lips. She's got that look on her face, like she knows something I don't. I do not like that one bit.

"Okay, and why did this news need to be told face-to-face? Could've just told Wells to tell me." I look back and forth between the two of them. "Something else you wanna tell me, Pops?"

"I want you to be nice to her," he says, like I'm not a nice person. "Drop the asshole attitude so you don't run her off."

"This better not be another matchmaking attempt. I told you after Leah that I was done with that shit. I don't need another woman to rip out my kids' hearts—"

"Watch your mouth," Momma chastises, shaking her head like she's disappointed in me. Even though she was really the one that taught me the worst of the words I know.

"Yes, ma'am." I wink at her, and it makes her smile even wider.

"Going over to watch my grandbabies," she tells me as she kisses me on the cheek. "We'll come see you for lunch."

"Thanks, Momma."

I'm going to have to figure out something else soon. I can't keep having her watch my kids every day. She's getting too old, and she deserves to enjoy her retirement, not work through it. And those kids are work.

Jolene is six, and Wade is five, and they both run around this damn ranch like they own the place.

"It's not a setup." Pops sighs once Momma has left the house. "She's young. But she's one of the very few applicants we got that had any experience with animals. I wanted someone who knew what the hell they were doin'."

"She from around here?" I take another drink of coffee, letting the life-giving drug burn its way down my throat.

"She's from San Francisco."

I damn near spit this coffee all over Momma's clean linoleum floor.

"And she's moving to bumfuck nowhere, Montana? To work on a ranch?"

"She wanted something new — a change of pace, she said."

"This'll do it."

"Be nice to her."

I grunt. I'm not an asshole; I'm just not one for small talk. I'm here to work, get my people to work, and go home at night to be with my kids. I'm done trying to make friends. And I don't need some little girl moving out here thinking it's gonna be a mountain vacation.

"I'm serious, Rhett. Be nice to that girl. Hardly anyone applied, and no one applied with the type of background we need. She's it." He makes a cut-off motion with his hand and then gives me a look. His eyebrow raises up toward his hairline.

"It's not gonna be my job to be nice to her," I tell him. "It's Wells'."

Pops sighs but lets me have it because I'm right.

Wells is in charge of all those animals, and I'm in charge of the working ranch. The ranch that makes us the money that allows us to keep Addie's dream alive. The ranch that will pay the city girl's paycheck.

"Wells better not dip his wick."

I laugh.

"Christ, Pops. What's her name?" Rinsing my mug, I set it on the top rack of the dishwasher.

"Poppy Sharpe."

"Age?" I ask, seeming uninterested but actually curious about how young this girl is. Moving by yourself to the middle of nowhere isn't for the faint of heart. I wonder if she has a family that she's leaving behind.

"Twenty-six."

Christ. A decade younger than me. She's practically a toddler.

"I gotta get," I say with a sigh. "Animals aren't gonna feed themselves. When's she coming?"

"Today. This morning, actually," he says, an ornery smile appearing on his mouth as he goes back to his paper.

"Nice," I deadpan. "Had to tell me at the last minute?"

"Didn't want you trying to stop the good things I set in motion for this business."

"*My* business, I'll have you know," I toss over my shoulder.

"Whatever." He brushes me off. "I ran it before you,

and your granddaddy did before me. I won't let you run it into the ground!" he calls out after me.

I can't help but slam the door as I stomp on my way out like a petulant child. He hates everything about what I'm doing to the family ranch. He hates that we take in rescues, rehabilitating them or giving them a good place to roam and sleep until they pass. Hell, it's not my idea of fun. I didn't do it because I think it's a blast.

I did it for Addie.

I love Pops, and he loves me. We get along most days. He might not agree with everything I'm doing, but he does agree that it's mine. The rescue is just a touchy subject — for all of us. When something is so strongly connected to someone you loved, it tends to leak into everything around it.

Shoving my hat back on as I step out into the rising sun, I breathe in the fresh air. Nothing like the smell of cow shit in the morning to wake you up. The view from this house is nothing but valley until it hits the mountains at the edge of our property. We have over one hundred thousand acres, with all of our houses spread out on the ranch but still within walking distance.

This one is the hub of activity just because it sits closest to the main barns — and has Momma's cooking. Once my kids get up, she'll bring them over and start working on breakfast for everyone. But I'll be a couple of hours into work by then, sweating my ass off, I'm sure.

It's supposed to be scorching today, even with the cool mountain wind whipping through the valley. As I walk off to the first job of the day, I can't help but dread meeting the girl from California. I already have an idea of what she's gonna be like, and I don't like it.

City girls think it's all hot cowboys and cute animals, but this shit is hard work. And the men are pigs. I groan. I'm gonna have to tell these men she's off-limits. No fucking around between the staff. But with her being the only girl on the ranch, it's gonna be like throwing her to the damn wolves.

"I'm already tired." I groan and stalk off to find my brothers.

CHAPTER THREE

Poppy

SAYING goodbye to those kids was far harder than I thought it was going to be. They're young, so they don't fully comprehend what's happening, but they know enough to feel how sad I was when I pulled them in for hugs. My throat constricted painfully as I tried to hold back the tears when their little hands gripped onto my shirt.

"You'll visit," Jessie said matter-of-factly, like she had already made the decision and she wasn't going to let me get away with never seeing them again.

"Of course I will." I glanced up at their parents, looking for confirmation that yes, I would be allowed to come back and see them.

"Anytime, Poppy. Seriously. Our home is always open to you." Amber smiled down at me.

I finally managed to wrangle my way out the front

door. But when I was halfway down to my taxi, Jessie came screaming after me, her face red with tears and her voice frantic.

"I almost forgot to give this to you!" she screamed, hiccoughing through the tears. "I made you...a key chain...for being my...best friend." I bit my lip and blinked back the tears. Saying goodbye to these kids felt like leaving a piece of my soul behind. No one ever tells you just how attached you'll grow to the kids you nanny.

The little beaded key chain is attached to my purse, and I play with the ribbons she tied all around it while I sit here on the plane. Something happened with our gate, so we've been stuck sitting on the runway for — I check my phone — thirty minutes now. The air-conditioning doesn't seem to be working either, and even though summers in Montana aren't scorchers, it's still hot as hell with all these bodies squeezed in like sardines.

I lean my head against the cool plastic next to the window and take some deep breaths. I've never been good with tight spaces, and the anxiety of this new place and new job on top of this really isn't helping me feel any better. God, this stagnant air! Can they not do something about this?

"First time in Montana?" the guy next to me asks. I look over at him and give him a small smile. I hate small talk. More than that, I hate small talk with men.

"Yep." I pop the *p*.

"What brings you here?" He's clearly a local, sporting a cowboy hat for absolutely no reason.

"Starting fresh," I tell him with a shrug. "Got a job on a ranch helping with rescue animals."

"The Blacks' ranch?" His eyebrows raise so high I can barely see them under the brim of his hat.

I roll my lips and nod. "Yep," I say, popping the *p* again. "You know the place?"

"Everyone does."

Our attention gets pulled to the front of the plane as it begins to move, pulling into a gate we've been staring at for half an hour. Finally, we're getting the fuck off this plane. I don't want to be dramatic, but I was going to die if we didn't soon.

"I'm from the area," he tells me while I try to yank my stuff from under the seat in front of me. "Grew up going to school with those boys and their sister. They're good people. They'll take good care of you."

Finally, my backpack dislodges from whatever the hell it was stuck on, and I'm able to pull it up onto my lap. I awkwardly try to put it on while not getting all up in his personal space.

"Well, that's good." Another polite smile. "But I can hold my own."

"I'm sure you can." There it is. That's what I was waiting for. The once-over. His eyes roam over my body like it's the *Mona Lisa*, appreciating every curve that's on display. "You look like someone who can put a man in their place."

"I can." I raise an eyebrow. "Eyes front, soldier."

He gives a hearty laugh and a little salute before standing to walk out into the aisle. Standing and stretching my legs feels amazing after being crammed into that tight little space. It's not that I'm tall; I'm not. I'm 5'5" on a good day. But I'm not the thinnest girl, and that makes it tough when all of the seats are built for a size two.

Don't get me wrong, I love my body. I have no qualms with the size eighteen I buy in jeans and the thighs that stretch them out. I just wish the rest of the world would get its ass in line.

"Good luck with your new job," he says, glancing at me one last time with humor in his eyes. "Maybe I'll see you around town sometime."

"Maybe."

I stare at his back as we walk down the aisle of the plane. He's not bad-looking, but the last thing I want to do is get involved with someone in a town as small as Cane Creek. Growing up in a town like that, I know how the rumor mill works. It'll churn out so much shit so fast that it'll make your head spin. And I'm here to start something fun, and men — in my experience — are not fun.

"Name's Gray."

He holds his hand out for me to shake once we make

our way into the airport. The sweet, air-conditioned space calms my nerves, and I take a deep breath. It finally feels like I can breathe.

"Poppy," I say as I take his hand. It's quick, though. I don't let it linger. "Nice to meet you, Gray. But the ladies' room is calling."

I break off from the direction he's walking and give him a little wave before turning my back on him. The last thing I wanted to do was walk all the way to baggage claim with him, making small talk while he worked up the courage to ask me for my number. So I take my time in the restroom to splash some cold water on my face and run a brush through my hair.

I'm starting to worry that I should've done something different with my hair. In San Francisco, no one bats an eye when you have fun colors in your hair, but in Cane Creek, Montana? It may draw attention I don't really want. And now I'm worried that my new employers are going to take one look at my peach-colored hair and regret hiring me for the job.

Too late now. And I like the way it looks next to my splattering of freckles and hazel eyes.

When I feel like it's been long enough that Gray can't possibly still be hanging around, I walk down to baggage claim. It was hard to fit my entire life into two suitcases, but I've done it enough in the last eight years that I made it work. I didn't want to show up with too much shit. I imagine they're already going to think a certain way about me since I'm coming from the big city.

Pulling hard, I manage to get both suitcases off the revolving belt. They fall to the ground with loud clunks, and my cheeks burn. Everyone around me is dressed in boots, jeans, and hats. My sundress and sandals stick out a bit more than I thought they would. I'm going to have to go shopping. I do not want to be labeled the high-maintenance city girl.

"Where to?" the taxi driver asks after loading my luggage into the trunk of his car. I'm sitting in the back seat, digging through my purse and backpack to try and find the hair tie I *swear* I left out of my luggage.

"The Blacks' ranch."

"The Rescue Ranch out on 43?"

I meet his eyes in the rearview for a second and give him a polite smile. "That's the one."

"Alright, then!"

The ribbons tied all over the key chain Jessie made me catch my eye. That'll have to work. I'm hot, and my hair is about to drive me insane. So I carefully untie one and then use it as best I can to tie my hair up and out of my way. It's not going to look the best, but I don't have the patience right now to care.

Especially when we pull into a long dirt driveway that leads us under a steel archway with "The Black Family Ranch" cut out of it. The mountains sit behind the expanse of farmland, and the sun is high in the clear blue sky. I gaze out at the massive trees that line the driveway and the animals grazing behind the wooden fences.

"Alright, miss," the driver says as we make a circle in front of a white two-story house. The front porch wraps around the entire thing, and there is a porch swing on either side, with a bright yellow wreath anointing the door in the middle.

I immediately want to drink sweet tea on this porch.

"This is it?" I ask, a little bit in awe of how cozy it looks. I don't know what I expected, but it definitely wasn't this.

And it definitely wasn't the attractive man leaning on the porch railing, watching me with a smile as I step out of the car.

"Hey, city slicker!" he calls as he walks down toward me. "Name is Wells."

His smile is warm, and I immediately like him. He looks to be my age or maybe a little older. His hair is a dark dirty blond, and his eyes are like chocolate. The corners of them are crinkled from the intensely happy smile painted across his mouth.

"Poppy," I tell him, returning his grin with my own.

CHAPTER FOUR

Poppy

"SO?" he asks, his hands on his hips as he looks over the land and then back to me. He keeps his eyes off my body, which I appreciate.

"So?" I ask, not sure what he's getting at.

"What do you think? Is it what you imagined?"

I look around, taking in the fresh mountain air and the noises of the animals. There's a faint smell of cow shit on the breeze, which just reminds me of my child-hood home. Just…way nicer. I come from a small town that's filled with meth heads and alcoholics. This place reeks of old money.

"Honestly," I say, looking back in his direction, "I'm not sure what I expected. But this is beautiful."

"Yes, it is. I've been lucky to call this home my entire life. I'm the youngest of the siblings. Rhett will be popping up anytime now, I'm sure. He's the oldest —

takes care of the working ranch side while I normally just work on the rescue animals. Hayes is around here, too, but we probably won't see him. My guess is he's off playing his guitar somewhere to piss Rhett off."

The humor in his eyes makes me want to laugh along with him. I can definitely tell he's the baby of the family. He has that look about him, and he just acts like he has less to worry about than a normal rancher might.

"We have another brother — Dean — but he's not around right now. And we had a baby sister, but…" He clears his throat and forces a smile. "Yeah, she's not around right now either. Anyway." He smiles as big as he can and waves his hands around him in a *look at this place* gesture. "Let's give you a tour!"

He grabs both suitcases by their handles and drags them up the dirt path to the front steps. I'm thankful he's taken both of them, even though I feel bad I didn't even try to take one back. But I'm tired, and that man is a cowboy. He has plenty of strength to get those things hauled up to the house.

"We'll put your shit, excuse me, *stuff* in the main house for now, get you introduced to Momma and Pops. Then after the tour, I'll take you to where you'll be staying on the property. I'm sure Pops told you, but you'll have your own place. We have some cabins scattered across the property, and we got one all cleaned up for ya." He looks over his shoulder and winks at me before yanking the screen door open.

"Momma? Pops?" he shouts at the top of his damn lungs once he's in.

And damn, it's even more gorgeous on the inside. His mom has it decorated like a home. There are warm colors and comfortable couches and chairs that I could sink into for hours while reading a book. She has pictures of her family on every wall, and the old wooden floors creak beneath our feet as we walk down the hallway and into the kitchen.

"Hi, Poppy!" An older man stands from where he was sitting at the table and walks toward us. His hair is all grey, almost white, and he's got an old pair of glasses hanging on to the tip of his nose for dear life. Wells looks exactly like him. They even have the same eye crinkles when they smile.

"Poppy, this is Pops," Wells says, bobbing his head between the two of us. "That's a mouthful."

"Homer Clyde Black the Fifth, at your service. But you can call me Clyde, dear." He takes my hand in his own, his work-beaten fingers wrapping tightly around mine in a comforting gesture.

"Clyde," I repeat back to him. "Very nice to meet you."

"Where's your brother?" he asks, dropping my hand to turn to Wells as he sets my suitcases by the back door.

"Which one?"

"Rhett. I told him to have his ass, excuse me," Clyde

says, briefly turning back toward me before continuing, "*butt* over here to greet our Poppy."

Our Poppy.

That feels nice.

"I really don't mind the swearing," I chime in, leaning toward the two of them. "I was brought up in the backwoods around a lot of boys who had no manners."

"Doesn't mean we can't try to have them now," Clyde teases, winking at me just like his son did a moment ago.

"Not sure. Last I saw, he was out messin' with the cattle fence out near the rocks. Probably got caught up. Where's Momma?"

"Ah," Clyde says, waving a hand in Wells' general direction. "Out with the kids somewhere. Who knows?"

"Alright, well, I'm gonna take Poppy here on a little tour around the ranch and then come back to grab her stuff." Wells opens the back screen door and gestures for me to go through it. "We'll be back in a bit. If Rhett shows up, send him down to the dogs."

"Don't let him run you ragged!" Clyde calls after us.

I laugh at Clyde and then do a little jog down the back stairs to catch up with Wells. We're heading out toward a barn off the back of the house.

"Much easier to travel by ATV," he tells me when I catch up. "We have a fuck ton of them, so we'll get you one to keep parked by your cabin. Help you catch a few extra minutes of beauty sleep."

"Thought you were going to try to have some manners," I tease.

He shrugs. "Figured you should probably get used to it sooner rather than later. Because once you meet Rhett, you'll be lucky to have a single sentence come out of his mouth that doesn't have profanity in it."

"I think I'll survive."

For the first time, he looks me over. But this doesn't feel like he's checking me out, more just appreciating the way I carry myself. He nods.

"I bet you will, Poppy. I bet you will."

He uses those strong rancher arms to rip back the barn door. It creaks and moans under the stress of moving, and damn, do I relate to that. Once I hit twenty-five, it was like my joints decided to just quit on me. If it's not one thing, it's another.

"So…ATVs, huh? A fuck ton of them?"

"Yep!" He pops his *P*, too. I like this guy. "This one'll be yours. Got it cleaned and gassed up."

Pulling back the tarp that was over it, he reveals a gorgeous Polaris RZR. I'd know one anywhere. We used to have these and would drive them around our small town at night to get to each other's houses. I distinctly remember smoking weed for the first time out of a Coke can in one years ago.

"Ever ridden in one?" he asks, pulling me out of my memory bank.

"Many," I tell him, climbing into the passenger seat. "Drove them, too."

"Well, aren't you full of surprises, city slicker?"

I roll my eyes at that little nickname I've been given. If only he knew where I grew up…saw the double wide I called home. He might look at me a bit differently.

"Where to first?" I buckle in and relax back in the seat, making sure to tuck my dress between my thighs. Don't need that blowing up in the wind.

"Figured I'd drive you around the main spots on the property." The engine revs to life, and I throw my head back in laughter when he wags his eyebrows at me. "Then I'll take you down to the dogs!" he shouts over the roaring noise.

We jerk forward and roll through the barn doors before he guns it, and we're off. I grab onto one of the bars above my head and smile wide. This is the most fun I've had in ages, and I've only been here for all of twenty minutes. I can't imagine how the rest of my time here is going to go, but I'm incredibly optimistic.

I'm giddy from it all. This is turning out to be the best decision I've made for my life. The scenery opens up as we race through the fields, showing off the blues and pinks of the mountains as the sun shines down on them. The animals graze, and the birds fly overhead.

Wells' cologne mixes with the hint of gasoline from the ATV, and I breathe it in like it's life-giving.

Yeah, I think to myself as I tilt my head back and close my eyes against the sunshine. This is where I belong.

CHAPTER FIVE

Rhett

I CAN HEAR them before I see them.

I'm running late — got caught up fixing a fence out on the edge of the property and lost track of time. Not that I was thrilled to meet the new face of Rescue Ranch, but that doesn't mean I wasn't going to attempt to be professional.

But as I round the barn, I can hear both of them cackling and hollering like they've not got a care in the world. That's the first thing that pisses me off. The second thing is that when I get to the open barn door, the sight I'm greeted with is the bottom curve of her ass as she bends over to help Wells up.

He's on the barn floor, laughing so hard his face is red and his eyes are shut. The new litter of puppies we took in are trying to lick him to death while they nip at

Poppy's ankles. She's laughing so hard there's barely any noise coming out, just a wheezing cough as she tries to catch her breath.

And all the while, that sundress she's wearing is so short that if she moves, I'm going to see exactly what panties she chose to wear this morning. And that infuriates me. Who does she think she is? Showing up on her first day dressed like that...for a *ranch*. Even the little sandals she's wearing make me mad. What if she stubs her toe? Rolls an ankle in a hole some animal has dug?

"Wells!" she squeals as she wipes her eyes and then tries to lift him up again. Her hands are all over him, touching his shoulders, gripping his biceps as she tries to yank him up off the ground. But he's too far gone in his laughter to even make an effort. He falls back fully on the floor.

"What the hell is going on in here?"

My voice booms through the barn, scaring her and the puppies. They run off, but she spins so fast to face me that she trips over one of them and flails. Down she goes, right on top of Wells as his arms open, and he tries to catch the brunt of her fall. Her legs fly up into the air — and yep, there's her panties. White cotton-looking things with strawberries all over them.

Christ, give me the fucking strength.

They both burst out laughing again as Wells envelops her in his embrace, and they roll to the side to deflect her fall. Her hair is falling in her face and out of the...what the fuck. Is that a bow in her damn hair? One, her hair is a pinky-peach color, which you don't see around here. And I don't like at all that I find it pretty. Two, she has it tied up with a silky-looking ribbon that lets pieces of that pretty hair fall into her gorgeous face.

I bite the inside of my mouth hard enough to taste blood and fist my fingers until they go numb.

I will *not* find the new hire attractive. I will not. I will not. I will not.

Someone needs to tell that to my dick, though, because it needs to deflate. Immediately.

Walking over to both of them, I reach out and grab hold of her wrist before she can protest and yank her up off my youngest brother. Her laughter dies when she lands on her feet, and she's quick to try and right her dress and her hair.

"Hey, brother," Wells says, climbing up off the floor. The way he looks at me is annoying, with that little smirk like he knows exactly how I'm thinking right now. "This is Poppy."

She outstretches her hand with a big smile that lights up those hazel eyes of hers. Her lips are full and pink, and *fuck*, they look like they'd be fun. Pushing that thought as far away from my mind as I can, I look down at her hand and then back up to her face before crossing my arms. Her hand falls back to her hips as she looks me over.

"Rhett, I presume?" she asks, her voice all sass, even though the kind smile hasn't left her face.

I grunt.

"Told you he was a ray of sunshine," Wells says. "Just be glad I'm your boss and not him."

He winks at her, and she snorts out another little laugh. When her eyes swivel back to me, they hold a lot less kindness. Good. Keep it that way. She doesn't need to like me; she just needs to do her job.

"My ranch," I state.

"Yes, Rhett. We all know." Wells makes a show of pounding his chest and speaking like a caveman. "Me Rhett. Me owner. Me big, strong man."

Poppy laughs again, but this time, she has the decency to cover her mouth like she needs to be at least a little respectful in front of the boss.

"You bring different clothes?" I ask her, ignoring my brother.

"You think I can't work in a sundress?"

"I *know* you can't work in a sundress unless you want to have all the men around here running after you, waiting for a swift breeze to blow it up."

"That what you'll be doing, cowboy?"

Wells snorts.

I grit my teeth and breathe in deep through my nose.

"Yes," she says, rolling her eyes. "I brought plenty of work clothes. Don't get your panties in a knot. I'm an adult, not a child."

"Could've fooled me."

Her face turns bright red, and all semblance of teasing leaves her features. Her fists clench, and I know she's about to let me have it. I know the signs of an angry woman. I've experienced them enough. I raise an eyebrow, egging her on and waiting to see what damage she can do.

"Alright, enough." Wells steps between us, clearly seeing the same signs that I do. "Don't be a dick, Rhett." He gives my chest a little shove, and I take a step back. It frees my head of her floral scent and clears my thoughts.

"You done fuckin' around?" My eyes are on him now.

He rolls his eyes and sighs. "Yes. I'm about to take her over to the cabin. Just gotta run back to the main house to grab her stuff."

"Good." I turn my attention toward her. "This is a real job. This isn't someplace you can come hang out at for the summer and chase cowboys. This is hard work, dirty work. My father seems to think you're the best person for this job. I expect you to prove that to me."

"Roger." Her voice is devoid of any warmth.

"This ain't the city—"

"Save it," she interrupts. "You got your point across.

You don't like me. You think I'm some stupid city girl come here to get a good lay from a cowboy. That's not who I am, and that's not why I'm here. I'm not afraid of hard work and getting my hands dirty. So save your breath."

We stare hard at each other for a moment. Why does she have to be so goddamn beautiful. After a long few seconds of Wells looking between us to see which one is going to make the first move, I sniff and tip my hat in her direction.

"Lovely to meet you."

"Wish I could say the same." The way she crosses her arms under her breasts makes them push up and together, giving me too good of a view. Between that and the way she flashed me her panties earlier, I'm done for the day. I need to cool the fuck off. Or chop some fucking wood. Something to get my mind off this woman.

I turn on my heel and stalk out of the barn, the heavy clomp of my boots the only sound in my wake. I know they're going to talk shit about me the moment I'm out of earshot. I'm used to it, being the asshole of the family. But you have to be when you're a single dad running an entire goddamn ranch that doesn't seem to want to make money anymore.

But what I'm not expecting is to hear them both burst out laughing once I'm around the corner.

"What a grump!" I hear Poppy say between the fit of giggles.

"Told ya," I hear Wells say right before I'm out of earshot and walking up the hill. Yeah, I definitely need to chop some damn wood. I need to sweat this whole interaction out of my system.

CHAPTER SIX

Poppy

WELLS TAKES me to my new home, a little cabin tucked against a tree line with a gorgeous view of the mountains from the front porch. He leaves me pretty quickly to get settled in, and I have to say, I appreciate it. I've had a long-ass day, and after that interaction with Rhett, I'm ready to have a drink and go to sleep.

"There are some groceries and a couple bottles of wine in the kitchen. Didn't know what you liked, but didn't want to leave you stranded without food before you could get into town." Wells smiles at me as he stands in the doorway and watches me look around. "Coffee's in the pantry, and cups, plates, silverware, all that good stuff is easy to find. Have a good look around, call me if you need anything. Oh, and Momma cooks breakfast and snacks for everyone pretty much every day. And you can always find a fresh jug of lemonade or sweet tea in the fridge. Help yourself — everyone else does!"

With that, he winks and is off, jogging across the wide expanse of land back to wherever his house is. They all live on the ranch, scattered about and in separate houses, but all within the confines of the land itself. Not that I blame them. This place is beautiful, and the land — for them — is free. Why not build on it?

Wells showed me around a lot of the ranch, pointing out where all the different animals are kept and where I'd be spending most of my time. Since I have the most experience with dogs, that's where they're going to start me. They have about a dozen at the moment, not counting the seriously cute but troublesome litter of puppies that so viciously attacked us earlier.

Which reminds me of the interaction with Rhett. Immediately, I start searching for the wine because that man has me all kinds of shook up. He looked at me like I was the shit on the bottom of his cowboy boots. Which is a shame because that is probably the most attractive man I have ever laid eyes on.

I find the wine and violently shove the corkscrew in.

They shouldn't make men that attractive; it gets a girl's hopes up. From his thighs like tree trunks to his broad shoulders and unkempt dark hair that stuck out from under his cowboy hat...that man is built like sin. He's nothing like the bodybuilders I'm used to who spend too much time in the gym honing their muscles.

No, Rhett's muscles are built from hard labor and a strong work ethic. And there were so many things I could picture him doing to me with those rough hands and big muscles. Hell, I bet he could throw me around a bedroom pretty easily, and that's not an easy feat.

I swallow a hearty gulp of wine, cringing at the burn on the way down.

Luckily, he opened his mouth and ruined all of those fun daydreams. It's for the best, really. The last thing I want to do is have a crush on my boss or, worse yet, jump into bed with him. That's not what I came here for. And for him to insinuate I did...god, what an ass.

"Did you bring any other clothes?" I mock him out loud to the empty cabin, my voice whiny and nasally. "Did I bring any other clothes," I say again, in my normal voice this time, as I toss one of my suitcases on the bed.

Setting the bottle of wine down on the nightstand, I unzip the suitcase and throw back the top. I gesture to the whole thing that's stuffed to the brim with jeans and old T-shirts.

"Yes, I brought other clothes, you insufferable asshole."

I groan and start unpacking, murmuring and mumbling to myself in between long pulls from the wine bottle. Sure, there are dresses and short shorts in this suitcase, but I'm not going to be working 24/7. I will have nights and weekends off, and maybe I'll want to go out! Maybe I'll want to go to the movies or a bar and have a drink with the locals.

I throw my last pair of jeans into the drawer and shove it shut with my hip. The damned thing sticks, making my hip bone connect with the old wood way harder than I intended. So after cursing the old dresser sufficiently, I decide to have a snoop through my cabin.

The wine decides to come with me, and even though my brain knows better than to get drunk the night before my first day of work, Rhett's bad attitude has me taking another sip. But the little house they put me in is perfect. It's one story with one bedroom and one bathroom.

The kitchen is my dream. It looks like a little cottage fairy lives here. I run my hands along the butcher-block countertops and then check the few plants they have lying around to see if they need water. But they're all good. Someone must come here and take care of them.

The living room boasts a huge fireplace that someone is definitely going to have to teach me how to use. There's a pile of wood sitting next to it, but I have not the slightest clue of how to make a real fire. The last place I lived just had gas, and all I had to do was flip a switch.

All of the walls are painted a creamy white that makes the whole place feel clean, while the furniture and blankets thrown around everywhere make it feel cozy. I open a few windows to get the breeze blowing through the house and then fall back onto the worn leather sofa. I carefully set my wine on the floor next to me and close my eyes.

It's so quiet. I can hear the tree frogs and the crickets come out as the sun starts to set. I'm exhausted, and the silence is letting me slip inside my head. I really hope I made the right decision. Until Rhett reared his ugly head today, this had felt like the best decision I had made in years.

There's that anxious but excited feeling in my stomach that's churning, and my shoulders feel like ten years of stress has been lifted. There's something about this place, from the moment I set foot on the property, that has done something for me. I'm far away from friends and family, and I'm completely starting over, but I'm not scared. I'm excited.

I know Wells is going to make a great friend, and from the way his dad was when I met him, I know this family is welcoming and loving. Despite the asshole that says he's the one in charge. That attractive, built like a brick shit house asshole that has decided to come in and kill my high, squashing it like a bug.

The sun sets, and the breeze gets cooler. I look up to make sure I've hooked the lock in the screen door, then tug one of the blankets over my body. I should get up and move into the bedroom, but I'm so comfy. And it's still so early. I can just take a nap and then move into the plush king-size bed in a bit.

Oh, and I can have a little snack after my nap. He

said they got me groceries, and I'm pretty sure I saw some tasty-looking frozen lasagna in the freezer when I was snooping. My stomach growls, but I ignore it, rolling onto my side and snuggling up against the couch cushion, choosing sleep instead.

CHAPTER SEVEN

Poppy

THERE'S a loud pounding coming from somewhere that wakes me up and scares the absolute shit out of me. I go to roll out of my bed and turn my alarm off but roll off a couch instead, whacking a wine bottle and spilling it all over myself and the cream rug it was sitting on.

I am not in my bed. I am in Montana, on my new couch, and the fucking sun is up.

"Shit," I swear under my breath.

"*Shit* is right!" the asshole shouts from the screen door. Not that he needs to shout because, like I pointed out, it's a screen door, not a solid one. He may as well be shouting in my damn ear.

I stumble to my feet, picking the wine bottle up off the floor as I do. The mess is catastrophic. Why did I have to pick the red wine? Jesus fucking Christ. My first day and I'm already late, *and* I've managed to inflict property damage.

When I finally make it to the door, Rhett's angry eyes give me a once-over and widen when they land on the wine bottle hanging at my side. His nostrils flare, and his face turns a hilarious shade of red. If I wasn't looking at my very angry boss, I'd probably be laughing. But I do not have a death wish.

"Are you a *drunk*?" He practically spits when he says it, and I watch his hands curl into fists. It makes the muscles on his forearms bulge in delicious ways.

I sigh.

"No, Rhett. I am not a drunk. I had a few sips last night, fell asleep before I could set an alarm, and then when *you* decided to scare the shit out of me, I fell off the couch and spilled the wine."

One dark eyebrow lifts up as he looks me over.

"You're still in your dress."

"Thank you, Captain Obvious."

He grunts. "Get dressed."

I give him a salute and then not so subtly slam the door in his face, clicking the dead bolt into place and feeling very good for doing so.

"You know I have the key, right?" His voice sounds bored, but I can practically hear that stupid little proud smirk.

"That's an invasion of privacy!" I shout back before I mumble, "Get fucked," under my breath as I stalk away to get cleaned up. I'm hoping even if I do it quickly, he'll get the hint and go away. I can make my own way to the rescue barn. I don't need his supervision.

But when I open the door, dressed in more work-appropriate clothing, he's still there. But thankfully, so is Wells.

"I tried to stop him," Wells says, rolling his eyes at his brother.

"I'm really sorry, Wells." The door shuts behind me. "I was just so tired. I passed out on the couch and hadn't set an alarm. It was actually my intention to get up and eat dinner before going to bed, but...clearly, that didn't happen."

"You haven't eaten?" Rhett asks, his voice deep and stern. I glance in his direction and see him staring me down, that scowl he loves so much giving him a groove between his eyebrows.

"I'm fine," I state, turning back to Wells. "What's on the agenda today?"

"Eating," his brother says.

"Didn't ask you." I refuse to look at him, but Wells just looks back and forth between the two of us, like he's afraid to jump in between.

"Don't care," Rhett states. "Get your ass on the horse."

"Excuse me?" I glance around and see a horse tied to a tree, its head bent down as it sniffs and bites at the grass. "No." I shake my head. No way in hell I am getting on that horse with Mr. Grump. No. We would have to sit way too close to one another, and I know my lady bits cannot handle it.

I walk off toward my ATV that Wells left here yesterday instead. If he wants me to eat, he can ride along with me and pick up his damn horse later. I'm not getting on that thing.

"Poppy Sharpe!"

He just full fucking named me.

"Rhett Black!" I shout back over my shoulder, but when I glance back, he's hot on my heels, his arms pumping and his legs carrying him much faster than mine can carry me. "What are you doing?"

"Rhett!" Wells says in a warning tone.

But it's too late. Rhett grabs my arm, spins me around, and lifts me up over his shoulder like I weigh as much as a feather. My face smacks against his ass before I can catch myself, and that is *not* how I wanted to be introduced to it.

"Rhett!" Wells yells again, harsher this time. "You can't just go cartin' her around like she's one of your kids!"

Kids? He's a dad? Who in the ever-loving hell could put up with this man long enough to have babies with him?

"Watch me," Rhett grunts.

"This is so incredibly unprofessional," I say, my word laced with annoyance.

"Like that dress you were wearing yesterday?" he asks, tossing me up onto the horse, who is clearly used to his shenanigans. That poor thing doesn't bat an eye. "Or how you were late and covered in wine this morning?"

He looks up at me, the sun shining through the trees to shine on his brown eyes that almost look like honey in this light. I can't help myself — I make a face at him. I don't stick my tongue out, but I may as well have, it's that childish of a face. And lo and behold, the grump can smile. Because he drops his head and laughs into the horse's neck before grabbing hold of the saddle and hopping up behind me.

I can't lie, it's pretty hot how easily he can just swing me and himself around like that. It's not too hard to imagine what he could do in the bedroom with muscles like that. And that smile — shit, it could drop all the panties in a three-mile radius.

"This here's Lucille," he says as his warm body settles flush behind my own. "She's a good girl, aren't you, pretty one?"

He pets Lucille's neck, invading my space even more than he already is. His voice has changed, too. He's kind to Lucille, speaking to her in a low, sweet voice. Guess he just saves the disdain for me. I must bring it out in him. Lucky me.

And between hearing that sweet voice say *good girl* and the scent of his cologne wrapping around me, my girl bits are on full alert.

Like I said, gets a girl's hopes up.

His thighs settle snugly against my own, and his arms wrap around my torso to hold on to the reins. I have to fight every instinct in my body that's shouting at me to lie back against his strong chest. I bet it would feel nice there. Instead, I lean forward, trying to get myself some damn space.

"Quit shiftin', woman," he grits out in a hushed tone.

My face flushes, and I bite back a smile.

"Guess I'll take myself to work, then!" Wells shouts. I whip my head to look back at where he's just laughing and shaking his head at us. This must be normal for Rhett. I have a feeling he isn't used to not getting what he wants.

"Looks like it!" Rhett shouts back, then gives Lucille a quick nudge, and she starts off toward the main house.

"Where are you taking me?"

When he speaks, his breath feathers against my hair, and his chest vibrates against my back. "Up to Momma's house to feed you."

I have never had such a strong reaction to a man before. Especially one that makes me hate him so much every time I see his face or hear his stupid voice. I shouldn't be so attracted to someone who is so very clearly *not* attracted to me. Hates me, in fact. I could kick myself for falling asleep last night.

Not only because Rhett was the one to wake me up and see that I was late and covered in wine but because I let Wells down. He expected me to be there to help him, and I wasn't. This is not the first impression I wanted to make.

CHAPTER EIGHT

Rhett

I DON'T KNOW what the hell came over me. But I don't like it.

Sure, I was angry when I showed up at the rescue barn bright and early, only to find Wells there feeding animals alone. It only took me a few seconds to realize she hadn't shown up and a few more seconds to storm off back toward Lucille. Wells had come yellin' after me, but I kicked her into gear, and we were off.

I think he shouted a few choice words in my direction, but I was too angry to care. It's disrespectful and just plain lazy to not show up on your first damn day. After the way she showed her ass — literally — I wasn't about to let her get away with making a fool of my business.

But then I showed up and saw her covered in wine and still dressed in the outfit from yesterday. Her eyes were tired, and her hair was a mess. My protective instincts kicked in. I wondered if we had hired a drunk, something this ranch could not afford another one of. My brother's face had flashed before my eyes until she opened her damn mouth.

And when I found out she hadn't eaten? That was it. It was like a light had switched on inside of me that wasn't going to turn off until I saw her put some damn food in her mouth. Working all day on an empty stomach that had only been supplied wine was just plain stupid. I wasn't going to have my employees passing out on the job, no matter how much of a pain in my backside she was.

The girl needed a damn meal.

She shifts on the saddle again, and I stifle a groan.

Why the hell did I think it was a good idea to lift her up, letting that sweet scent of hers invade my space, and toss her up on Lucille? And why did I think it would be a good idea to saddle up behind her, pressing our bodies so close there's not a hair's breadth between us?

Stupid, stupid man.

Because now I'm stuck grinding against her gorgeous ass for the entire trot up to Momma's. Cultivating some mental images of my great-grandmother is the only way I can keep my dick under control. The last thing I need is to get a hard-on with the new hire on my horse.

"You have kids." She states it like it might be a joke.

I grunt in affirmation.

"So you're married?" Her voice goes up at the end like she would be truly shocked if the answer was yes this time.

I grunt in negation.

"Can you do anything but grunt?" She swings around, whacking me in the face with that pink ponytail that smells like vanilla.

I smack it away. "Yes, I have children. No, I am not married."

"Girlfriend? Baby mama?"

"Ex-wife."

"Oh, that makes far more sense." She snorts.

"Somethin' funny?"

"Honestly, I couldn't imagine a woman putting up with you long enough to have babies." She sighs, and I watch her knuckles tighten on the saddle. "Sorry, that was rude. I've been told I have no filter."

I grunt again. "Takes more than a sassy comment to hurt my feelings, poppyseed."

Thankfully, Momma's house comes into view quickly, and both of my children come running out onto the front porch and down the dirt path, eager to meet the new face. Pops has been talking her up since she got here, and she's now the kids' newest obsession.

"Your hair is pink," Jolene states as she looks up at Poppy with wide eyes.

"Pink is her favorite color." Wade stands behind his older sister, his hand clasped on the back of her dress.

I hop off Lucille and tug Poppy off after me. She immediately walks over to them and sinks to one knee. I try very hard to not notice how those jeans hug that peachy ass as she walks and how the top of the denim gapes at the top when her shirt rides up. It gives me a thin strip of skin to ogle at before her voice cuts through the fog.

"Pink is my favorite color, too!" she says. "My name is Poppy. What's yours?"

"Jolene. But everyone calls me Jo. Except for Daddy, he calls me Joey."

"Is that his special nickname for you?" Poppy asks, her voice lowered like they're sharing a secret. Joey's head bobs, making the buns on top of her head bounce. Momma is always puttin' her hair up like that. Space buns, Joey calls 'em.

"My name is Wade," he says, stepping forward and holding out his hand, ever the gentleman.

"Wade!" Poppy grabs his hand in hers and shakes it wildly until he's in a fit of laughter. "It's so nice to meet you!"

"Joey, go on in and tell your grammy that Poppy here needs to eat something. We'll be inside in a second."

"You got it, Daddy!" She salutes me and grabs Wade's hand, dragging him behind her as she screams at the top of her lungs for her grammy.

"We don't talk about their momma," I tell Poppy as she stands from her squat.

"Not my business to talk about." She looks at me seriously, but just earlier, she said she didn't have a filter, and around my kids…that worries me.

I nod after a moment and then lead her toward the front steps.

"How old?" she asks, squinting when the sun hits her face. It makes her nose crinkle and shows off those damn freckles. I add those to the list of things I shouldn't be noticing about the new girl.

"Joey is six, and Wade is five. Irish twins."

She laughs, but it's not in her normal mocking way toward me. When I meet her eyes, she's got a genuine smile on her face.

"Was Wade a happy accident?" She nudges my bicep with her shoulder. Heat explodes at her contact.

"You could say that."

"So, we don't talk about their mom. Can I ask what happened there?" When she sees what I'm assuming is a grimace on my face, she backtracks. "Sorry, like I said, no filter. You don't even know me. You don't have to tell me anything."

I shrug. "She wanted Montana, 'til she didn't. She

wanted me, 'til she didn't. And she wanted those kids, 'til she didn't."

"She's not present at all?"

"Not unless you count a card every birthday and Christmas with a five-dollar bill inside that's always sent from some new address. We never know where she is, and we like to keep it that way."

She hums and kicks the ground as she walks. "That's sad. They seem like great kids."

"I'd like to think so."

"They're very cute. Although, I'm sure they both have an ornery streak in them that runs wild." She laughs to herself. "They look like you," she tells me, smiling up at me again.

That smile is dangerous. That smile holds promises that I want to explore. Things that I haven't explored since Wade was conceived. Hell, probably long before that. Being a single dad doesn't leave much time for dating, not that I'd change a thing for those kids. They're my whole world.

But with their momma leaving, and both them and the ranch becoming my full responsibility, I swore off the trouble that women could bring into my life long ago. My dick still doesn't seem to get the memo, though, as she crosses her arms and pushes her tits together under the grey T-shirt she's wearing.

I grunt in response to her statement.

"Always grunting," she says as I open the front door

for her. The smell of biscuits wafts toward us as she pauses to really look me over. I stand a little taller under her gaze, and I'm ashamed to admit I think I puffed my chest out a bit. "I'll crack you sooner or later, Rhett Black."

Damn, if I'm not tempted to let her try.

CHAPTER NINE

Poppy

SEEING Rhett in dad mode is off-putting.

And by off-putting, I mean extremely adorable and way too sexy for my lady bits to handle. I swear my ovaries liquify watching how his kids dote on him and how he gives them all the love in the world right back. It's such a dichotomy, watching him with me and then watching him with them. He saves all of his sweet smiles and calming voice for kids and animals, it seems. I'm the lucky one that gets all the grunts and raised eyebrows. Oh, and the manhandling. Can't forget the manhandling.

He leans over and picks Jolene up, her awkwardly long and lanky limbs wrapping around him like a koala. Both of the kids are at that age where their limbs are outgrowing their bodies, making them look like little aliens running around.

"Hi, Poppy!" his mom says, her warm smile and even warmer eyes greeting me as she reaches out for a hug. She wraps me up tight, and the smell of flour invades my senses. I blink back tears when the memory of my grandmother pops into my mind. "My name is Katherine. And I heard you met Clyde yesterday?"

"I did." I smile at her when she pulls away and walks back over to the countertop where she's rolling out some dough. "Nice to see you again," I tell him when he pulls out a chair for me at the table.

"Take a seat, take a seat," he says before patting me on the shoulder and helping me scoot the chair in. "Katherine here makes enough for the entire farm damn near every day. And today, we have biscuits and gravy with eggs and sausage. Oh! And her homemade strawberry jam."

"Wow." I take a deep breath as I look over the spread on the table. "I'm already late. I can just grab something to go..." I really don't want to. I want to sit here and enjoy their family presence, soaking up all the love they have to offer. And I really, really want to eat everything on this table. It's been since the airport yesterday that I had anything, and good god, this food looks and smells amazing.

"Fine by me," Rhett mumbles from where he holds Jolene on the other side of the kitchen.

"Mumbling is bad manners," she scolds him. Her

little finger pokes at his chest, and her eyebrows furrow.

"Yes, it is," he agrees. "My apologies, sweet girl."

"Don't be silly!" Katherine says, wiping her hands on her apron. "You had a long day yesterday, and Wells has been doing this by himself for quite some time. He'll be okay if you sit down and eat for a minute."

Her eyes swivel to give Rhett a look, but he just rolls his eyes and sets Jolene back on the floor.

"Fine. Eat your breakfast. Then get yourself over to the rescue barn. Those animals aren't gonna take care of themselves." He kisses his mom. "Momma, thank you for the breakfast. It was delicious."

"Ignore him," Clyde tells me under his breath as he fills up a plate for me and the back door slams shut behind Rhett. "He's always been a bit of a grump. But the last few years haven't been easy on him."

"Why not, Gramps?" Wade asks, sticking his body in between us. He steals a biscuit off my plate, and I swat playfully at his hand. He disappears under the table in a fit of giggles.

"Quit eavesdropping. And quit callin' me Gramps!"

Clyde smiles at me and sits back down.

"I always said I'd be a grandpa. And the moment Jo over there started calling me Gramps and got a reaction out of me, it's been Gramps ever since."

It's all in good humor. I can tell he loves these grandkids of his more than life itself. He sets Jolene up on his lap and pushes some flyaways back into her space buns. She is a spitting image of Rhett, and it's so strange to see his hard features on a small girl. But she's gorgeous, with that brown, wavy hair with highlights from spending so much time in the sun and her light brown eyes.

Goodness, she's going to be a heartbreaker.

My stomach growls, making Wade and Jolene laugh.

"You sound hungry," he says from under the table. "Want your biscuit back?"

His hand pops out from under the table, holding half a biscuit with little teeth marks on it from where he's eaten the other half. His fingernails are dirty from playing on the ranch and just being a little kid.

"We have plenty," Clyde says at the same time I say, "Um, no, thank you, Wade."

We sit like that for twenty minutes. I eat my breakfast, the kids play around the house, and Clyde and Katherine chat with me about my life. They're interested in my schooling, what I do for fun, and what made me want to move to Montana.

I answer everything truthfully, telling them I've never really felt settled, that I wanted a fresh start somewhere with plenty of room to grow — mentally and career-wise. Not that I'm throwing my hat in the ring to become anything more than what I am to this ranch yet, but that thought had crossed my mind when I accepted the job. Surely there's room to grow here. Over two hundred thousand acres...there's got to be a reason to keep me on.

"Momma!" another brother — I'm assuming anyway — shouts as he runs in through the front door.

"Uncle Hayes!" the kids shout in unison, running through the front hallway. I hear them tackle him and a loud *oof* as they knock the wind from him.

"In the kitchen!" Katherine shouts back, rolling her eyes when she catches me smiling. "That boy," she says to me. "Nothing but trouble."

Hayes walks in and gives his mom a kiss on the cheek before turning to say hi to his dad and seeing me sitting at the table. His whole demeanor changes, and I can just *see* the troublemaker flirt come out in him. Katherine is right — Hayes is all trouble.

Hayes has the same color hair as Wells but just a bit lighter, like he spends more time in the sun. But from the guitar hanging at his back, I doubt he works as hard as the other boys. Something tells me he likes to slack off a bit. His eyes are hazel, like my own, and when his hands make contact with the table to lean into my space, I can't help but appreciate the strong hands and fingers from all that guitar playing.

But still, something is missing. Wells and Hayes are attractive. Very, very attractive. Katherine and Clyde gave them some golden genes. But when they look at me and are all smiles, I miss the way Rhett scowls. I don't know what that says about me, but the well-mannered boys just don't do it for me.

I like 'em a little mean.

"And who might you be?"

"That's Poppy!" Jolene says.

"She's new!" Wade says as he crawls back under the table, presumably to finish his biscuit in peace.

"And her hair is pink," Jolene adds.

"I see that," Hayes tells them, never taking his eyes off me. "I like that peachy color. Reminds me of the Montana sunsets."

I can't help it — I laugh right in his face, spitting pieces of biscuit out as I do. He blinks and leans back.

"I'm so sorry," I tell him while chewing.

"Serves you right." Clyde grins and leans back to open his paper. "Don't flirt with the new hire."

"Don't flirt with anyone that works here!" Katherine scolds.

"She's the only female. I promise, the others are safe." Hayes grins and sits next to me. "So, Poppy the peach from the city. I'd be happy to walk you down to the rescue barn when you're finished. I can give you all the dirt on my brothers on the way."

"Thank you," I tell him, grinning when his eyes light up. "I would actually love that. I think I need to level the playing field when it comes to the grump."

"Rhett?" he asks, a look of interest sparking. "He's harmless. But I have plenty I can tell you."

Hayes stands and holds out his hand for me to take. I do, and he tugs me up.

"Will you come to dinner on Saturday?" Wade asks, peeking out next to my legs.

"You should," Clyde says, turning a page. "Katherine always has the boys over on Saturdays, and we'd love to have you."

"And we go out afterwards." Hayes wags his eyebrows. "Drinkin' and dancin'. What do you say, Poppy the peach from the city?"

I roll my eyes at the nickname. Bit of a mouthful.

"Alright, if you're sure." I look over to Katherine, but she just gives me another one of her bright smiles.

"You are always welcome here, sweetheart. Breakfast, lunch, dinner, snacks…whatever your heart desires. Want to come over just for some company? Well, Clyde and I are here for that, too. You just bring yourself and that pretty smile."

"Thank you." My eyes water, but I manage to blink it away before anyone notices. Damn, these people have known me for less than twenty-four hours, and they're already making me feel more at home than I've ever felt.

"Ready?" Hayes asks, walking toward the front of the house. "We'll have to walk it. I don't have my ATV with me."

"As long as you don't throw me up on a horse, I don't care how we get there."

He gives me a confused look but shakes it off as I take his arm.

"Bye, everyone! Thank you for breakfast!" I call over my shoulder.

A chorus of *byes* and *your welcomes* follow us as Hayes and I step out into the morning sunlight.

CHAPTER TEN

Rhett

"YOU GONNA HELP or just sit there and play that damn guitar?"

Hayes sighs and sticks the guitar pick between his lips as he sits the guitar to the side and stands.

"Poppy didn't yell at me like this," he complains, sticking the pick in between the strings. "I want to go work at the rescue."

I laugh, but it's anything but humorous. Hayes is a hard worker when he wants to be, but never in the way we *need* him to be. I need him to be here, on this damn ranch, helping me keep us all afloat. But he wants to pursue music. He's good — damn good. But I can't afford to lose him here. Not with Dean gone.

"Poppy isn't your boss. I am. And you wasted so much time over there with her and Wells that we're a good chunk behind on this damn fence repair." We don't have any animals grazing over here, but come the end of summer, we'll be switching some of them back to this side of the property, which means this needs to be done by the time the weather starts to change.

"What do you think of her?" he asks as he comes over to help.

I grunt. "S'alright."

Out of the corner of my eye, I can see the smirk across his face.

"Yeah, she's alright." His smile grows wider. "Peachy hair and a peachy ass. Just my type. Think I should make a move, maybe see if she's down for a little romp in the hay? I bet city girls like her have no clue what it's like to ride a cowboy." He makes a stupid gesture like he's ridin' a bull that I do not find funny.

I toss the fence stretcher and sleeves to the ground and turn to face him. He's already grinning, like he knows exactly what buttons he pushed and exactly what I'm gonna say.

"Hayes."

He looks at me, a faux expression of innocence painted all over his face. Little shit.

"Is that a no?" he asks, his eyebrows bunched together.

"That's a hell no. Off. Fucking. Limits."

He rolls his eyes.

"Why so protective? She's the first woman we've had working at this ranch since Addie." He laughs and shakes his head. "You really think you're gonna be able to keep these men away from her?"

"I have so far," I all but growl.

"When I left the rescue, she had four of the guys in there introducing themselves and looking her up and down. They're like lovesick little puppies."

I swear under my breath and pick the shit up that I threw on the ground and toss it into the pack on Lucille. Taking my gloves off, I tell Hayes that I'm done for the day.

"You *just* got my ass up to help. What's got you all riled up?"

"I didn't say you were done," I tell him. "Finish the last of this line so we can get a leg up on tomorrow. I'm going to make sure the new hire isn't just sittin' on her *peachy ass.*"

"Oh, so you just get to ride off home and enjoy your evening while I'm stuck out here working my ass off?" He puts his hands on his hips like an incredulous teenager. "It ain't even quittin' time! And who gives a flying fuck if she's taking it easy her first day?"

"Hayes, you showed up late and sat on your ass for half the day." I hitch up onto Lucille and smile down at him. "I think you'll be okay for another hour."

"Hour, my ass. This'll take two at the least."

"Longer if you keep gabbin'."

Lucille anxiously stomps her feet below me, reading my energy. I don't know what's come over me, but this woman sets my goddamn nerves on edge. Hayes flips me the bird, but I just give him a tip of my hat before letting Lucille take off.

The sun is setting when I make it over to the barn. The warm light pours out from the open barn door, and I keep Lucille back. I'm only here to check in… observe. I'm ready to kick those boys out if they haven't let her be. It's about time she does her damn job and earns the paycheck that my pops is so adamant we can afford.

But I don't see anyone hanging around. I don't even see Wells. It's just Poppy in there, taking care of the dogs that will hopefully find a home soon. I watch her as she takes each dog out on one of our long leads, testing their behavior and their recall with a treat once they've hit the end of the rope.

After they've pottied for the night, she plays with each of them, taking the time to work on some manners and some tricks. Some dogs are easier than others. She spends the most time with the puppies, taking them out individually to get them used to being independent. They don't quite understand the lead, but she teaches them that it isn't a chew toy and rewards them when they go to the bathroom in the grass.

I'm mesmerized as I watch her. Her hair is up in a messy bun on the top of her head, causing the shorter strands to fall down the back of her neck and the ones in the front to frame her face. She smiles, claps, and cheers the dogs on as they all go back to their spot for the night.

And once it's quiet, she goes to the one all the way at the back.

My chest gets clogged with emotion when I see her sit down and lean her head back on the hardwood. There's a dog in there that hasn't come out of her shell yet. A red pit that was found being dragged across a road, all because she was trying to pee and her shitbag owner didn't like it.

She came to us with needle marks on her inner thighs from the drugs they were pumping her full of, probably to get her ready to fight, and a demeanor that made you want to kill the man who had her. Wells was barely able to get her moved from the truck to the barn, worried she was going to hurt herself by thrashing around out of sheer terror.

Poppy takes the time to sit with her. She doesn't do anything else. Just sits. Waits. I can't see from here, but I imagine her eyes closed and her breathing slow and calm. She's waiting for that baby girl to trust her — to come to her on her own.

It reminds me of something Addie would do.

Us boys would come home from school each day, and we'd never know if Addie had been out rescuing some poor animal from the brink of death, only to nurse it back to health. She was always on the lookout for creatures she could save.

Even when she was at her sickest, she had a rabbit she had found with a broken leg in the backyard. Against all of our wishes, including her doctor's, she took care of that thing better than she took care of herself. Sometimes I wonder if she knew she didn't have a lot of time on this Earth, just like those animals who were sick and broken. So she tried to give them another shot at living — one she wouldn't get.

I know that's why Pops has such a hard time with this whole operation. He can claim that he just sees it as lost money all he wants, just me sinking money into something that isn't worth it. But I know better. I know the memory of Addie is alive in every animal we bring back — whether it's a dog, a cow, or a damn hairless chicken. We rescue them all and give them a place to rest because that's what Addie would've wanted.

She couldn't stick it out any longer, so I keep her memory alive the only way I know how.

"Ready to go home for the night, girl?" I bend over and pat Lucille on the neck. She huffs as I stroke the soft hair of her mane.

Glancing up at Poppy one more time, I wonder if that poor dog will give in tonight. But I don't stick around to see. I have a horse to put up and kids to take off my momma's hands.

CHAPTER ELEVEN

Poppy

"POPPY?" I hear my name being called from outside the barn. I've been working with the scared dog in the back of the barn all morning while Wells takes care of the rest of them. Once everything was done, he left to help his brothers with the fence. He told me to take a break and eat some lunch, but I told him I wanted to stay here. We're finally gaining some traction, and I'm hoping she finally lets me pet her today.

I slowly, so as not to startle her, stand from where I've been sitting at the front of her little kennel area and walk toward the front. Katherine rounds the side of the barn with Jolene and Wade in tow.

"Hey, guys!" I greet them with a big smile. They've brought me lunch a few times this past week, and I've taught them some things about training dogs. With the well-behaved ones, that is. "Come to help me out again?"

"I'm so sorry to do this to you, sweetie, but is there any way you could watch them until Rhett comes back this evening?" Katherine's voice is strained, and I can tell she's not thrilled about asking me. Not because she doesn't trust me — but she's worried she's putting me out.

She absolutely is not. I may not be fond of their father, but I love them.

"Of course, Katherine. Is everything okay?"

She sighs and wrings her hands. "Clyde went out with the boys to help finish the last of the fence, and I've just got word that my friend in town hurt herself and needs to go to the hospital. She doesn't have any family, and I'm the closest friend she has…"

"Say no more. Go be with your friend. I will take care of the kids."

"Gosh," she says, looking relieved. "Are you sure? This isn't what we pay you for, but—"

I cut her off and lay my hand on her forearm.

"My last job was a nanny. I love kids. I promise I do not mind watching them until Rhett gets home for the evening." I smile down at them. "We'll have fun, right?"

"Maybe we can play with the puppies?" Wade asks hopefully.

"Oh, for sure. Let's do it." I wave to Katherine and mouth that they'll be fine as I follow them into the barn.

They run ahead of me, but before they can get too far, I stop them to set a few ground rules. Kneeling down, I make sure they're both paying attention. The last thing I need is for one of them to get hurt on my watch. That wouldn't win me any favors with the grump.

"Hey, guys. I know you've been around animals since you were born. But I think it's always good to have a little reminder that animals have boundaries, too. Right? We have to respect them and make sure they're comfortable when we are petting them and playing with them."

"Yes, ma'am," Wade says.

"And we stay away from the shy one at the back," Jolene reminds us both.

"Right," I agree. "Her name is Betty."

Jolene scrunches her nose at that. "I don't like that name."

I laugh. "Me either, really. But that's what she responds to, so we need to keep it. The less change, the better for her. Now, should we go let the puppies out to play?"

The rest of the afternoon goes by smoothly. They're great kids, and I find myself falling in love with their smiles and the laughter they treat me to all day. Once the puppies were wiped out from playing, they begged me to take them over to the other rescue animals. Jolene has a cow that she loves to visit, and her puppy dog eyes won me over.

I made sure all the dogs had what they needed, and then we set out for the special cow. We had a couple of hours before I expected Rhett and the guys to come back, and the place they wanted to take us wasn't too far away from the main house. I figured we would pet the cow and be back home before anyone else.

But that is not what Jolene had in mind, and damn it if I wasn't a sucker for that girl.

"Don't you love her?" she asks from where she sits beside me on the driest patch of grass in the field. "She's so sweet and cuddly."

The cow — Wendy — was thrilled to see Jolene. She wasn't lying — this was her special cow. And Wade loves her just as much. She came running up to all three of us as we approached, and when Jolene started working on the gate, I realized we were not just here to pet her from the fence. We were *going in.*

This is out of my depth. I've never supervised kids around farm animals, but they both seem so confident, and Wendy seems so sweet, so I think it'll be fine. I know cattle tend to be docile animals, especially if they are socialized with humans from a young age; it's something I learned while growing up. They could really be quite domestic.

And this one proved to be just that. For the past hour, we've been sitting here together in a heap of cow cuddles.

"Do you know we don't have a momma?" Wade

asks out of the blue. I'm leaning back on my hands, tilting my face up to the sunshine. When I look over at him, he's petting Wendy with the saddest little face I've ever seen.

Jolene's little braids fling around as she turns to look at him.

"Wade," she scolds. "We don't talk about Momma."

He sniffs and wipes his nose.

"Hey, it's okay. You can talk about whatever you want with me, okay?" I tilt his chin up and give him a smile. "And you do have a mom, Wade. She just isn't here. That's her choice, and it sucks."

Jolene gasps.

"You said sucks."

"I did. Don't tell your dad." I wink at her before turning back to Wade. "But you know what you do have?"

He shakes his head.

"You have a huge family that loves you dearly. You have a daddy that lives for you and plenty of uncles to keep you busy. You've got your grammy and gramps."

"And you?" Wade asks.

I shouldn't be surprised by that question. Both he and his sister have spent the entire week playing and talking with me. Kids latch onto people so easily. It makes my chest constrict, knowing that he's already fond enough of me to consider me part of his inner circle.

"And me," I assure him.

"You should marry our daddy," Jolene says, laughing when I swivel my head and go bug-eyed.

"Excuse me?"

She laughs even harder when my voice cracks as I playfully squeal at her. Wade joins in, and soon, they're both in a fit of giggles as they repeat over and over that I should marry their father.

"You should!" Wade says between laughs.

"Marry our dad! Marry our dad!" they chant.

I start tickling them, and Wendy gets sick of the commotion and groans as she lifts her heavy body off the ground. And just when I think they're going to laugh so hard they pee themselves, I hear Rhett shouting my name from the gate.

"Where in the hell have you been?"

I bring my hand up to shield the sun from my eyes and realize he is not in as playful of a mood as we are. He's stalking across the field like he's ready to light one of us up.

"Playtime's over, kiddos," I grumble right before he walks up.

"I've been looking for you everywhere!" he shouts, his face red and angry. The kids immediately take shelter behind my body like I'm going to save them from the wrath of their dad.

Not a chance in hell, kids.

"Joey, Wade…go over to your Uncle Hayes. I need to have a chat with Poppy."

"But, Dad!" Jolene whines.

"We weren't doing anything wrong!" Wade shouts, on the verge of tears again.

Rhett sighs and composes himself.

"You know you aren't allowed to come out here without an adult."

I scoff. "What am I? Chopped liver?"

His eyes close like he's summoning the patience to deal with me. He probably is. He doesn't like me much, but I don't really care.

"It's not her fault," Jolene says, stepping out to take her dad's hand. "Don't yell at her. Promise."

"Promise, baby girl. Go to your uncle, okay? I'll meet you back at the house."

My stomach is doing somersaults and churning. I feel like I might throw up. Not only is Rhett incredibly hot when he's all surly and angry, but I'm also a little afraid of him.

Is he going to fire me?

Shit.

CHAPTER TWELVE

Rhett

I'M FUMING. I can feel the heat radiating off my body. We finished the fencing early and came home to an empty house and quiet yard. Pops had tried calling Momma, but she didn't answer and didn't reply to any of our texts. Turns out she forgot her damn phone. Pops found it layin' on the bench next to the front door.

The panic seized my chest. I've never not been able to find those kids. My brothers and Pops kept me calm, telling me they had to be around the ranch somewhere. Which I knew. I knew that. My brothers and I disappeared for hours on end as kids. So I knew there was no way they were actually *gone*. But that doesn't stop the feeling of terror sweeping through you.

And when I saw all of them lying in the field with Wendy, the fear went away and was swiftly replaced with anger. Anger because it was Poppy who had taken them from where I knew they would be. Anger because those kids knew they weren't allowed out in this field with these animals without an adult. And while Poppy is legally an adult, she's not got a clue how to protect those kids from animals like this.

I hear Hayes and the kids start a race back to the house, and once I can't hear their footsteps anymore, I know they're far enough away from me to break my promise.

"What the *fuck* were you thinkin'?" I crowd into her space, but she doesn't relent. If anything, she leans into it.

"I was *thinkin'* that your kids wanted to come see a cow. I was *thinkin'* that I'm an adult, and I know how to take care of kids. I was a nanny before this, and I grew up with a gaggle of kids around. I'm not an idiot, Rhett. Don't treat me like one."

Her hands go to her hips, and she stands there defiantly. Her face is tipped up to meet mine, and the setting sun makes her eyes look more green than brown. And that peachy hair is falling out of her braids and into her face. Her eyes narrow like she's just waiting for me to fight back, to tell her she's wrong and that she is actually a child. She's looking at me like she *wants* the fight. My cock stirs.

"Poppy, you don't know the first thing about taking care of kids around farm animals. Dogs? Sure. I'll allow it. But when you're taking my kids into the middle of nowhere, without letting anyone know where you are, around animals that can kill you if they get the mind to—"

"It's a fucking *cow*!" she shouts. "God!" Her hands jut out and shove me hard on the chest. I take a step back, more so from the shock that she just shoved me than the force of it. Although, damn, she's pretty strong. "Why do you have to be such a dick?"

"Did you just shove me?"

She shoves me again.

"Yes!"

I can't help it… I laugh.

She groans. "You are seriously so infuriating."

"Look, I'm sorry for getting so angry," I say, trying to quell my laughter. "But you can't do that shit until you know your way around the ranch and the animals better."

"I do not accept your apology." Her arms cross in front of her chest, drawing my attention down from her face before I can stop myself.

God, that body. She has curves for days, and I just know she's soft in all the right places underneath those clothes.

"See something you like?" Her voice drips with venom. She does *not* like me. Not that I blame her. I've not been nice to her a single time since she arrived. What would there be for her to like?

I grin and make a show of looking her over. Should I

be more professional and bring my eyes straight back up to her face? Most definitely. But there's something about her attitude that's addicting. I like pushing her buttons. So I take my time and let my eyes linger in all the places they've wanted to for the past week. And then when I finally meet her eyes, they're heated.

She's pissed. My dick is throbbing, and I try my hardest to quell it.

I grunt and raise a shoulder, trying to look unaffected.

"Fuck. You. Rhett Black. Fuck you." She starts to walk away but turns around to deliver another blow. "You are welcome, by the way, for watching your kids."

"Hey," I say, grabbing her by the arm. She swings around and tugs her arm free. "Do you understand what I'm trying to say here?"

She gives me a look like I've grown another head.

"Yeah. That grunt was loud and clear."

"No, I mean—" I sigh. Shit, I've stepped in it. "I mean about my kids and the big-ass animals you know nothin' about."

"Loud. And. Clear." She gives a mock salute and turns on her heel. Her jeans grip her ass as she walks away, and I tilt my head to the side to get a better view.

I wonder if she even knows how to get back to the house. I should probably go after her, make sure she gets home okay. I shouldn't just stand here and watch her walk away, loving every single second I get of watching that ass sway.

But if I do go after her and walk her back to her cabin…I'm worried about walking away. Her sweet face, spicy attitude, and perfect body are a triple threat. I haven't felt like this around a woman in too long. I don't trust myself.

I don't trust my cock. It sucks all the blood from my brain, not leaving a lot of critical thinking skills. And when I think back to how adorable they all looked lying in the field together, laughing and tickling each other, my heart lurches. Their momma never took the time to love them like that, doting on them and giving them the attention they deserve. But Poppy did. Poppy has been.

Momma told me they've been spending lunch together every day, and every day, Poppy answers all their questions and teaches them how to be with the dogs. She's been nothing but nice to my kids and my family, and here I am, shoutin' at her and making her so angry she shoves and shouts at me.

God, I'm an ass.

She reaches the gate, looks around, and then takes off in the opposite direction she should be going. I drop my head back and sigh.

"Lord, give me the fucking strength." I take a deep breath and set off after her.

CHAPTER THIRTEEN

Poppy

GODDAMNMOTHERFUCKER.

He is an insufferable ass. I take back my apology for saying no woman could stay with him long enough to have babies. Because I don't even know how anyone could stay long enough to get naked with the asshole.

I look both ways, remembering the way we came from when the kids and I walked over to this field. But I think, unless I'm incredibly turned around, which could very well be the case, that my little house is to the right. I'm not very sure about that, but I refuse to seem like I don't know what I'm doing after that little rant he went on about me not being grown up enough to handle his fucking kids.

That stung. That stung, a lot.

I know I've always been looked at as too young and too this and too that. Being the baby of your family means they don't understand your boundaries or that you are actually a capable human being. There's always the stigma of being the youngest. While I took advantage of this throughout my years in high school, I'm a little over it as of late.

And to say that while also looking me up and down like I was something he wanted to take his time eating... God, I hate him. I hate him. And I refuse to admit that him shrugging after looking me over also hurt. Because that look in his eye was heated, so I refuse to believe he's actually unimpressed. If I do that, my self-confidence will take a massive hit, and no man is going to be the cause of that.

"Poppy!" he shouts.

I can hear his heavy footsteps jogging toward me. I pick up my own pace, practically speed walking to get away from him.

"You've said all you needed to say!" I shout back. "Leave it be, Rhett!"

"So I should just leave you walkin' the wrong way?"

Shit.

I stop, and he plows into me from behind.

Hah, that's what she said.

"Fuck's sake, Poppy!" He grabs onto my arms to keep me from toppling over, and I very quickly right myself and yank free.

"Leave me alone." I grunt out my frustration and start walking in the opposite direction.

"Just let me walk you home, you infuriating woman!"

"I'd rather chew glass, thanks."

"Poppy," he groans, catching up with me easily with those long, strong legs of his. Christ, even when I'm furious with him, I can't stop my mind from going to the gutter.

Ugh, who am I kidding? My mind lives there. Rent-free. Utilities? Paid for. Internet and cable? Wouldn't dream of paying for it.

"I can either walk with you or walk behind you. Whichever you prefer."

"I prefer not at all," I grumble.

"I prefer behind you." His tone is playful, but I am not in the mood.

I remain silent.

"Come on." He sighs.

"No, Rhett," I snap back as he walks up beside me. "You come on. Ya know, I don't feel I've done anything to warrant your anger. Other than having pink hair and accidentally oversleeping on my first day. But only one of those is cause enough for you to reprimand me."

"I—"

I cut him off. "I'm not done. I may be, what? Five years younger than you?"

"Try a decade." He scoffs.

Oh, that's surprising. This man does not look much over thirty, let alone closer to forty. The manual labor of working on a ranch has been very, very kind to him. I eye him out of my peripherals but soldier on.

"But that doesn't mean I'm a child. I grew up in a small town surrounded by farmland. So while I may not be as knowledgeable as you, I'm not an idiot." I tug out my French braids and run my fingers over my scalp. This man is giving me a headache. "I'm an adult, with childcare experience, who was asked to watch your kids for one afternoon. I love those kids. I wouldn't let anything happen to them, and I need you to trust me on that."

He grunts. Just freaking *grunts*...

So I give up and resign myself to walking in silence the rest of the way to my house. Clearly, he's not going to let me walk alone, and I'm not going to try and hold a conversation with someone who only communicates via grunting like a caveman.

The little house comes into view after a tense walk, and I couldn't be happier. It was cooler today, so I left the windows open, and the string lights they hung outside for me cast a warm glow over the little porch.

"I think I'm good from here," I tell him, gesturing to where we can both clearly see the house. But he won't stop walking, just trudging on like he's determined to drop me at the damn door.

"Made it this far," he says in a quiet voice. "May as well walk you to the door."

I roll my eyes but let him. Not like I could stop him

anyway. This man doesn't give up. I've shouted at him and physically assaulted him. At this point, I'm genuinely surprised I still have a job.

"Why didn't you fire me?" I ask when we walk up the front steps.

"Why would I fire you?"

I give him a look. "Because you showed up at my front door the first morning I was supposed to be working and saw me covered in wine. I was incredibly late. And then, if you remember, just a while ago, you laid into me about taking your kids into a cow field."

"Because I overreacted about my kids and because one fuckup doesn't mean you should lose your job."

"Meaning your mom and dad said no."

He laughs. "Something like that." He rubs the back of his neck and reluctantly meets my gaze. "The ranch needs you. Wells needs you. He's been doing this alone for too long, and it's startin' to wear on him. Poor kid needs a life outside this ranch."

I nod.

"Okay, then."

He crosses his arms under his pecs, which make his biceps bulge and puts his strong hands on display. I can't help but let my eyes wander over his body, just like he had done to me back in the pasture. Where I'm soft and curvy, this man is hard and straight. Broad shoulders, strong torso, and thick thighs are proof that he works hard.

When my eyes finally make their way back up his body, I find a little glint in his eyes. He's been watching me soak him in. But when he steps closer, crowding me toward the front door, I get a little wary. My body is screaming yes, but my mind has alarm bells going off.

The scent of sweat, leather, and a hint of laundry detergent fills my senses, making those alarm bells a bit quieter. There's a cool breeze that sweeps across the porch and makes a few pieces of his hair fall into his eyes. I fight the urge to push it back because that is *not* what employees do to their bosses. Those brown eyes bore into me, and I can't look away, no matter how badly I want to.

My back hits the screen door. There's nowhere for me to go. He's stalked me into a corner with no way out. My heart is pounding in my chest, and I can't take a deep breath. Meanwhile, he just smirks down at me, his eyes moving from my lips to my eyes and back like they can't decide what they like the look of better.

"Poppy." My name sounds delicious on his tongue. "See somethin' you like?"

"I do," I admit.

He pushes closer, his hips bumping against my own. His arms unfold, and his hands can't decide where to go. They sit on his hips and then move quickly like they're going to grab me before getting shoved in his pockets. I put one of my hands behind my back, making my chest push forward a little as I search for the doorknob, while the other goes to his jaw. The scruff bites at my fingers, and my clit pulses when his mouth opens just slightly.

He leans in like he's going to kiss me. God, I want him to.

"But this thing right here, " I tell him as I run my thumb over his mouth, "ruins everything else about you."

Before he can say anything, I twist the handle and curl around the door to slip inside.

"Good night, Rhett."

The screen door shuts, and I close the wood door, completely shutting him out. I even go as far as to dead bolt it, hoping that it'll stop me from opening it and jumping into his strong arms just to find out how good of a kisser he is.

Slowly, I lower my forehead onto the door and wait to hear him walk away. It takes a minute, but eventually, his footsteps recede, and I can breathe again. Turning and slumping to the floor, I bang my head behind me on the hardwood.

"Stupid, stupid, stupid, Poppy."

CHAPTER FOURTEEN

Rhett

I WALKED STRAIGHT HOME last night, bypassing Momma and Pops' house to pick up the kids. They could wait. They wouldn't even miss me. Throwing open the door, I ran up the steps and jumped in a shower of water so cold it may as well have come from the damn Arctic.

But it didn't help. My cock was still throbbing painfully as the cold water beat down on it. After a minute, I gave up and turned the water up until the entire bathroom filled with steam. When my hand wrapped around the base of my cock, I hissed at the pleasure.

I pictured Poppy the entire time. The way her ass looked under her dress, the strawberry panties she was wearing, the way her hips ground against me on the horse. Her eyes, her lips, her breasts...everything was flashing in front of my eyes as I tugged roughly on my dick.

I came so hard I thought my knees were gonna give out. Wouldn't that have been a way for someone to find me. Dick in hand, knocked out from coming so hard I hit my head on the tile. Christ.

I have got to get a damn grip on myself. I cannot be lusting after that poor girl. The last thing she needs is her boss, an old man — a single dad, no less — hitting on her while she tries to do her job.

But the way she touched my jaw and looked over my body had my mind on the fritz. I wondered if she was wet for me and what she'd taste like once I got my tongue between her thighs. A girl with a mouth like hers would sound the prettiest as she screamed out my name.

"Daddy, is Poppy gonna be at Grammy's?"

I'm jolted from my memory and look over to see Joey popping her head around my bedroom doorframe. Her hair is in a mess of a bun on top of her head, hanging on for dear life as she tilts her head to look at me.

"I'm guessin' so."

"I like her," she says as her eyes light up. She dips her head back out into the hallway while her little fingers still cling to the frame. "Told you she'd be comin'!" she shouts down the hall.

"Hey, Joey!" I call out to her before she can run away.

"Yeah, Dad?" She pops right back in, her little bun wobbling to the side.

"Make sure you don't bother Poppy while she's workin'."

"We don't. She likes us." Her matter-of-factness makes me grin.

"That might be the case, pumpkin, but she's tryin' to work. She has a job to do, and she can't be watching you and your brother every day."

She sighs and, with all the attitude in the world, leans a hip against the doorframe as she crosses her arms.

"She doesn't watch us. Grammy does. We take Poppy and Uncle Wells lunch."

"Well, maybe y'all should stop doing that every day. Let Poppy and your uncle do what they need to do."

"Well, maybe you should talk to Grammy. Because she's the one takin' us over there every day." Her little eyebrows raise up, and damn if I don't see myself in the way she acts sometimes.

"You're kind of sassy."

She smiles and pushes her nose in the air.

"I know."

And then, like a bolt of lightning, she's gone, calling after her brother. I quickly finish in the bathroom, brushing my teeth and running my fingers through my hair. I'm tempted to do something with it, maybe actually run a comb through it or use that pomade shit Hayes got me two Christmases ago. It's just been sitting there untouched ever since.

I sigh. Fuck it. I pull it out of the drawer and put a little in my hand, rubbing them together before messing it around in my hair. It settles into a bit of a style, and eventually, I just give up.

"Let's go!" I shout through the house.

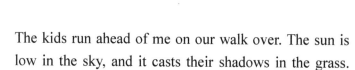

The kids run ahead of me on our walk over. The sun is low in the sky, and it casts their shadows in the grass. God, they're cute kids. I know I'm biased, but these kids have my heart.

I always knew I wanted kids. Growing up in such a tight-knit family can make you feel one of two ways: you strongly want that in your future, or you don't. Dean never has, but the rest of us always did. I swallow the bad taste in my mouth when my thoughts turn to Dean.

We have given that boy so much...

So much time and so much money and so much help. And every time, he just throws it away, swallows whatever sorrows he has with a bottle of the cheapest liquor he can get his hands on.

"Hurry up! We're gonna be late!" Wade shouts back at me.

I just laugh. "Go on, then. Run if you want! I'm comin'."

We are not going to be late. We're going to be early, but keeping these kids away from their grandparents is like pullin' teeth. On their first day of kindergarten, I thought Momma was gonna have to sit with them all day at school. They were bawling and hiccoughing, tearing my heart right out of my chest with each breath.

I watch them run inside, and I'm not long after them. The kids are carrying on with their uncles in the living room while Pops takes up his normal seat at the table, paper in hand. And then I see the flash of pink hair, and my whole body reacts. My cock remembers what we did last night, and he's ready for round two. And this time, he wants the real thing.

She's got half of her hair pulled up, and the rest sits in waves at her shoulders. The oversized white T-shirt she's wearing is almost see-through, and her jeans are so tight they make her damn ass look like an apple that I desperately want to take a bite out of. I run a hand through my hair, making sure the wind hasn't messed it up too badly, but then I remember I've got that shit in it, and I've probably just made it stick up in ways it shouldn't.

I regret the pomade.

"Alright," Momma is saying to her. "So you've put

in the cornmeal and flour. We just need an egg and a cup of buttermilk."

Poppy moves over to the fridge and grabs what she needs. Momma supervises as she cracks the egg and pours the buttermilk. I haven't seen Momma let anyone cook in this kitchen since Addie, and my heart is damn near tugged up through my throat. But the thing that hurts the most is when Poppy turns around to say something to Pops, and I see what she's got tied around her waist.

Her eyes glance up and see me standing there like an idiot, just starin' at her. My eyes flick from her pretty face down to her waist. And I'm torn. I'm torn between loving that image and hating it.

"Rhett?" she asks, her cheeks pink and her eyes bright. She's blushing, probably thinking back to what happened between us last night. But my ears are ringing, and my heart is a drum beating in my chest.

"Hey, baby!" Momma's voice breaks through the ringing. "We're making your favorite. Homemade cornbread."

"I was told to promise you it's not from a Jiffy box." Poppy's lips turn up into a smirk, but when I don't respond, she can tell something isn't right. "Rhett?"

I swallow, trying to find my vocal cords.

"Everything okay, son?" Pops asks, turning in his chair to face me.

I blink. "Take that off."

My voice has a bite to it, and no one but Poppy seems to notice. The color drains from her face, but she looks confused. Did no one tell her?

"The apron," I grind out. "Take that fucking thing off."

"Rhett Black!" Momma chides, her voice sounding genuinely shocked at how I'm acting. But both she and Pops should know better than anyone what this would do to me. Hell, they should care just as much as I do. And yet they don't, which makes it sting even more.

Poppy is frozen. Only her eyes move between the three of us standing around her. I need her to move. I need her to take it off. I can't stand to see her there, standing where Addie used to, wearing Addie's favorite apron.

"I said take it off!"

CHAPTER FIFTEEN

Poppy

I JUMP, startled at the new tone he's taken with me. I've seen angry Rhett, but this is a whole new side of him. This Rhett is triggered by me wearing this apron, and I am more than happy to take it off to get that look to leave his face.

When I first noticed he was here, I saw him just standing in the hallway, staring at me. My first thought was how good he looked. He was dressed in nice jeans and boots that didn't seem to be as worn as his other ones. And even his hair looked like he'd done something different to it.

But then the look changed and became something else entirely.

I untie it from around my waist and neatly fold it into a square before placing it in his outstretched hand. The tension is so thick in the kitchen right now you could cut it with a knife. His knuckles turn white as he grips that apron with so much force.

"Thank you," he grits out before turning on his heel and walking back through the hallway and up the stairs at the front of the house. Everything is quiet for a second, at least I think it is. My hearing is muffled from the force of the embarrassment and adrenaline.

"Poppy?" I look up to see Wells and Hayes standing in the archway that leads into the living room. The kids seem to be oblivious for once...thankfully. I couldn't handle it if they saw me get yelled at like that.

"What just happened?" I can barely find my voice, and it comes out as barely a whisper.

"It's our sister Addie's old apron. She passed a while back, and while it hit all of us hard, Rhett nearly didn't make it," Hayes says.

"The only thing that got him out of it was this whole rescue thing," Wells tells me. "Addie always wanted to rescue animals, so Rhett made it happen when he took over the ranch from Pops."

Clyde grunts. Like father like son.

"I should've said something about the apron, but I honestly didn't think he'd react that badly." Hayes clears his throat like he's holding back his own tears.

"He needs to realize that life moves on," Katherine murmurs. "Stubborn, heartbroken boy. I wear that thing all the time, and he never says a word."

"You're his momma," Wells tells her. "We should've known it would upset him. I'm sorry, Poppy."

My chest seizes with the pain he must've felt seeing me wear her apron. Tears roll down my cheeks without permission, and I quickly try to wipe them away. There's nothing I hate more than crying with an audience. But my heart aches in a way it hasn't for a long time.

"It's okay." I try my hardest to smile. Clyde just curses under his breath, something about how he didn't raise his boys to act that way toward a lady. But all I can think is that he had a right to act like that. I can't say I would've acted any different if I were in his shoes.

"Let's finish this up." Katherine tries to gently pull me in the direction of the counter, but I can't do it. I have to go talk to Rhett. I have to let him know that I didn't know, that I'm sorry for triggering him on a day that's supposed to be about his family coming together.

I sniff back my tears and smile in her direction.

"If it's okay, Katherine, I think I'm going to go find Rhett."

I don't stick around to hear what anyone has to say on the matter. I take off upstairs and eventually find him sitting in what I assume is his old room. He's sitting on the double bed in the far corner, running his fingers over the soft cream fabric of the apron. He doesn't even look up when I knock.

"Can we talk?" I ask.

At that, his head finally lifts. He's not crying, but he looks like he could.

"I, uh—" He sits up straight and takes a deep breath. "I had every intention of apologizing to you today."

"What for?" I step into the room.

"Last night. Yellin' at ya like you were a child." He huffs and rolls his eyes. "And then I go and do this."

I sit down next to him on the bed, pulling one leg up so that I can face him. He smells like he's freshly show-ered and wearing some kind of woodsy cologne. I want to bury my nose in his T-shirt and breathe him in.

"I didn't know it was Addie's," I say quietly. And then I push my luck. "When did she pass?"

"About eight years ago. She was seventeen. Lungs just couldn't take it any longer." He looks at me quickly before turning back away. "Cystic fibrosis. She needed a lung transplant, but those lists are five miles long, and nothing came in time."

I fight the urge to reach out and touch him. This isn't my grief, but I feel it like it is. I can feel the pain he's holding on to, and it makes my throat clog with emotion. Especially when he sniffs like he's holding back tears.

"For years, I prayed that another human being would die so that my sister could live." He gives me another humorless laugh. "How fucked-up is that?"

"You wanted your sister to live, Rhett."

"So badly that I wish someone else would lose

theirs. I watched her wither away right down that hall." He points out the bedroom door. "She was on meds to manage the pain, but once she decided she didn't want to hold on any longer, we all stood around her while she took her last breaths. We didn't want her to feel alone."

"I'm so sorry."

What else can I say? Sorry is so inadequate. Against my better judgment, I reach out. My hand lands on his strong forearm, causing his muscles to twitch. My very pale hand sticks out against his tanned olive skin like a beacon, but I like the look of it there. And when he reaches over and lays his hand on top of mine, my heart almost leaps out of my chest.

Then he's looking at me. Those burnt-honey eyes are locked on my own, making my entire body catch fire. His stare burns through me, and there's no water in sight. His jaw flexes, and that hand that was on top of my own lifts to push a stray piece of hair from my temple. He tucks it behind my ear and then lingers. The rough calluses on his palms rub against my cheek, making goose bumps break out on my arms.

"Poppy," he murmurs, that gravelly voice going straight to my center.

He leans forward, and I lose all ability to breathe. He's going to kiss me. His thumb runs along the line of my bottom lip and then drags it down, making my lips part. My tongue darts out and touches the tip of his thumb. A deep rumble comes from his chest, and then he's pushing it between my lips and into my mouth.

Like the greedy little whore I clearly am, I close my lips and circle it with my tongue before sucking it deeper. His eyes are hooked on my mouth, and that deep growl comes out of his chest again. When he looks up, he catches me staring.

"You good with that mouth, Poppy?"

I nod as he presses down on my tongue and moves his thumb farther back into my mouth.

"I knew you would be."

I'm so incredibly wet that I'm a little concerned there may be a damn wet spot on my jeans. My pussy clenches, and my clit thrums with the need to be touched or licked or *something*. Christ, the way he's looking at me. He wants to eat me up like a damn ice cream cone.

"Y'all almost done?" Hayes shouts up the stairs.

I jump, and Rhett rips his thumb from my mouth with an embarrassing *pop*. He stands up off the bed like I've burned him, and the apron falls to the floor.

He swears under his breath and picks it up, only to toss it down on the table next to us. I just sit there, stunned at what I let happen...stunned at how badly I wanted him to keep going.

"I'm sorry, Poppy. That shouldn't have happened."

And then he walks out, leaving me sitting on the bed a little hurt, a lot confused, and extremely turned on.

CHAPTER SIXTEEN

Rhett

THE ENTIRETY OF DINNER, I'm hard as hell and feeling like an ass. I keep trying to subtly adjust myself, but Hayes is onto me, having seen my state as I ran down the stairs to escape Poppy.

"I interrupt somethin'?" he asked with his stupid signature Hayes smirk. I almost punched him.

But now that dinner is over and my kids have run off with Pops to catch lightning bugs, my brothers are ready to go to the bar. Most weekends, I join them, just to make myself get off this ranch once a week. Tonight...I do not plan to go.

"Y'all have fun," I say quietly, hoping they won't see me trying to slink out the back door to join my kids.

"No way, big brother." Wells grabs me by the shoulders and steers me around, pushing me toward the front. "You can't miss Poppy's first night on the town."

"The hell I can't," I tell him. I avoided her throughout the entire meal. Ever since I shoved my thumb between those full lips, I haven't looked at her once. And I plan to keep it that way.

Mainly because I'm a coward. Partly because I'm still angry as hell at her for just existing.

Wells gives me one last shove, and I give in, defeated. Because honestly, the thought of not knowin' who she's talkin' to all night makes me want to punch a goddamn wall.

"You ever been line dancing?" Hayes asks her as we pile into his truck.

She immediately goes to the back, and I try to grab the front so I'm not stuck back there with her, in her space, my nose filled with her scent. But Wells knows what the fuck he's doing and runs in front of me to grab it first.

"You little shit," I growl under my breath. "I will get you back for this."

He just snickers and jumps in the truck.

"I haven't," she says as I climb in the back with her, a hint of nervousness in her voice. "Is that all anyone does here?"

"Nah," Wells says over his shoulder. "There's people dancing all sorts. But we'll teach you any line dancing they do if you're interested. Or Rhett will. Right?"

I grunt when he smirks at me.

"Maybe I'll choose a more enthusiastic partner."

That makes Hayes laugh.

"Oh, Poppy. You're gonna be covered up by enthusiastic partners. You're fresh meat."

That sentiment sours in my stomach immediately.

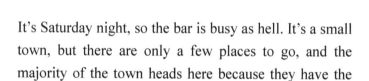

It's Saturday night, so the bar is busy as hell. It's a small town, but there are only a few places to go, and the majority of the town heads here because they have the biggest dance floor and the nicer beers on tap.

Hayes and Poppy go searching for a table while Wells and I try to fight our way to the front of the bar. I hate a bar that has seating all the way down. How is anyone supposed to order a damn drink if you've got people takin' up the entire fuckin' thing?

"So…" Wells says, leaning his elbow against the bar and wagging his eyebrows in my direction. "Poppy."

I grunt. "What about her?"

"You like her."

I get the attention of River, who's working behind the bar tonight. She smiles when she sees us and walks over. No wonder Hayes took off running with Poppy. He wouldn't want to be anywhere near River. I don't know what happened between them, but I know it wasn't good.

"She's alright," I answer.

Wells sighs, already fed up with me, as I order our drinks. But he's not gonna get shit out of me. Because there's a rule at the ranch: you don't get involved with people you work with. Not that it's an official rule, because, well, we haven't had this issue before. There's also the fact that she's a whole decade younger than me, and I have two kids that I take care of full-time. I can't drag her into that.

What happened earlier this evening was stupid and irresponsible. My head was all over the place from seeing her in Addie's apron, cooking with Momma, and I was filled with so many conflicting emotions that I couldn't sort through it. And then she came into that room, smelling like flour and whatever perfume she wears, and I just lost it. I couldn't help myself.

It won't happen again. It can't.

"You know you don't always have to be such an uptight asshole, right? You can let your guard down sometimes…live a little."

I grunt again.

"I know that Leah did a number on you, Rhett. She fucked you and the kids over, turned your life upside down right as all that Dean shit was going down. Hell, the whole family was turned on its head for a hot minute." The drinks get slid in front of us, and I nod my thank-you to River. "But we all love Poppy. And she looks at you like she's gonna tackle you in the dirt."

He grins and side-eyes me.

"That's because she hates me. She's probably waitin' 'til I turn my back so she can beat the shit out of me."

"Don't you consider that foreplay?"

I ignore him because once I see Hayes, I notice he's sitting by himself. Following the direction of his gaze, I find Poppy smack-dab in the middle of the dance floor, her hands all over a guy who looks very familiar.

"You let her go off with a stranger?" I growl as I slide in next to Hayes. I'll be damned if I'm puttin' my back to her.

"They aren't strangers. I went to school with Gray, and they met on the plane." Hayes rolls his eyes, then looks over at my tense form. A pit of anger and jealousy settles deep in my gut. "And you look madder than a snake."

"Don't know why he'd be mad," Wells says. "Told me himself at the bar that she's just alright. No interest in her whatsoever."

"Interesting." Hayes leans forward like he's telling a secret, but I can't take my eyes off the way Gray's hands are touching Poppy's waist. "Because when he came downstairs for dinner, he was sportin' quite the woody."

"Rhett Black," Wells says, doing quite the impression of our momma. "What in the world were you doing upstairs alone with that new ranch hire?"

"Fuck off," I spit in his direction. Then I turn to Hayes. "Saw River at the bar. Maybe you should go say hello."

His face drops and so does his playfulness. Instead, he becomes very interested in downing the drink in front of him. Which is stupid, seeing as he'll just have to go talk to River to get another.

"That was below the belt," Wells chides.

The song changes, and now Gray is teaching my girl how to line dance. And as soon as that thought enters my head, it's like a damn record scratch. She is not my girl. Why did I just call her that? Why do I feel this sudden possessiveness over her?

She gives him the biggest smile while they pull apart and come back together. Her feet are stumbling, but he catches her each time, which makes her head fall back in laughter. She's having the time of her life out on that dance floor while I'm dying a little on the inside just watching.

I want all of her touches and smiles. No one else deserves them. Hell, I don't deserve them. But I'm a selfish man, and I won't deny that seeing her touch another man has lit a fire inside of me. I want to claim her in front of everyone, throw her over my shoulder like a caveman, and take her home.

The beer tastes like shit going down because my

entire mood has soured. And I know what I'm about to do next is going to change everything about the way my ranch works. I know that I'm about to break my own rule, and I'm about to be the most unprofessional boss. But that doesn't stop me. It can't. My mind is already made up.

"You look determined," Wells says, a touch of humor in his voice.

"He is." Hayes lightens up a bit. "He's gonna go get the girl."

I set the empty bottle of beer back on the table.

I sigh.

I look at both of my brothers, who just smirk back at me.

Poppy glances over at me, catches me staring, and then blushes furiously.

"Fuck it."

CHAPTER SEVENTEEN

Poppy

I GUESS it was bound to happen, running into Gray in a town this small. When he came over and asked if I would dance with him, Hayes all but shoved me out of the booth. I had my suspicions as to why he wanted me to go with Gray so badly. These brothers are constantly fucking with each other, and I had a feeling he thought it would fuck with Rhett.

I'd be lying if I said I didn't want it to fuck with Rhett, too.

What he had done at his parents' house had me on edge. Sitting in the back seat of the truck with him was torture. And knowing that I now have to spend the entire evening with him, I'm afraid I'm not going to make it through without making a fool of myself.

I am not the girl that throws herself at men. If they don't want me, they don't want me. And that's fine. But I know Rhett wants me. You don't just go around sticking your thumb in people's mouths you *don't* want to fuck. But he's stubborn, and I'm sure he's not a fan that I'm so much younger than him. Or that I work for him.

So I'm just trying to enjoy myself with Gray. He may not look at me like we're just friends, but that's okay. I don't intend to see him that often, and I have three men with me that would probably beat him to a pulp if he did anything I didn't like. And it's just a bonus that we're right in the line of sight of Rhett.

Gray spins me out from his body and then tugs on my arm, yanking me back into him. I collide with his chest because my feet can't seem to keep up with this fast-paced country dancing. My eyes just so happen to check back at the table where I left Hayes. Like a magnet, I'm drawn straight to Rhett, who is looking at me like he either wants to punish me or fuck me.

I feel my cheeks heat, and it takes all my strength to tug them off his scowl. He hasn't shaved in a few days, and that beard is doing all sorts of wonderful things to my lady bits. I'm betting it would feel amazing as he ran his mouth between my thighs.

"You are just what this town needs," Gray says, smiling down at me from under his cowboy hat. He's handsome, but I just can't see anything past Rhett. I don't know when that happened, or how it happened so quickly, but that man is all I see.

"Oh yeah?"

"Needed someone new, someone fun to lighten everyone up around here."

I laugh and look down at my feet, hoping I can will them with the power of my mind to hit the correct steps.

"Not sure how fun I am. I'm an asleep-by-ten kind of girl now that I'm working all day on that ranch. I'm exhausted constantly."

"They workin' you too hard over there?" At first, I think he's still being playful, but when I look up, his eyebrows are drawn together in concern.

"What?" What a ridiculous thing to ask. "No. It's a good kind of exhaustion. I'm finally doing something that makes me feel like I have a purpose. It's nice working with my hands and my body. And they've been nothing but kind to me."

"Even Rhett?" he asks, his voice a bit louder than I wish it was. Especially when I notice Rhett has walked up behind him.

"Even Rhett, what?" he asks, grabbing Gray's attention.

"We were just talking about how kind you and your family have been," I intervene.

He grunts. Always with the grunting.

"Well, I came to steal you away. I think Gray here has had enough of your time." He places a heavy hand on Gray's shoulder, giving it a hard squeeze that makes Gray wince.

The butterflies in my stomach flutter around and wreak havoc.

"We're in the middle of a song," Gray bites back.

"Don't care." Rhett shrugs.

"Hey, it's okay." I smile at Gray. "I can dance with you again later."

"No, you can't."

I whip my head to Rhett, giving him a dirty look. There's no reason for him to be an asshole right now. Especially after I'd just sung his praises to Gray.

"Hey, man. Come on. She's having fun, just leave her alone."

The way Rhett sighs and laughs after Gray tries to put his foot down does something twisted to my insides. I shouldn't love this little show of possession, but I do. The rational side of me wants to end it, to show Rhett the door and spend the rest of my night with Gray just to piss him off. But the other side of me wants to see how hard he'll fight for me.

The latter wins out.

"Leave, Gray."

"You don't have to be an ass, *Rhett*."

"He does, actually," I chime in, reminding them both that I'm standing here. "It's his autopilot."

Rhett gives me one of his rare smiles, and hopeful flowers bloom where the butterflies were.

"Leave."

"Come on, Gray!" Hayes shouts from where he sits twenty feet away. "Let the man dance with the woman!"

Now everyone's eyes are on us. When I say Hayes shouted, I mean he *shouted*. Loud enough that his voice would carry over the music and reach us on the dance floor. I can feel my face heat, but Rhett just stands there, arms crossed, like he's not moving until Gray lets go. Which also makes me realize that I am still in Gray's arms.

I step back, and Rhett clocks it.

"Settles that," he says, taking my hand and tugging me off to another spot on the dance floor, far away from Gray and the guys he's been hanging out with. By the time we get over there, most people have decided to ignore us again, but I can still feel their eyes on me like I'm a fish flying out of water.

"You didn't have to make a scene," I grumble.

"You want to dance with someone? Dance with me." He pulls me in until our bodies are flush together, and his scent makes me dizzy. "You want to smile at someone? Smile at me."

Our eyes meet, and the intensity there scares me. It's like he's diving inside my soul, looking at every part of me, and carving out a space for him to exist.

"And if you want to touch someone, poppyseed? You touch me."

I melt a little at the nickname he's given me. So far,

I've only heard him give one to his daughter and to me. That makes me feel special in all sorts of ways. My thighs clench together, and my heartbeat races. A small grin settles on those perfect lips, and then he's twirling me out from himself, only to whip me back in.

This time, I don't stumble. I keep myself upright, hitting the steps just as I need to. His hand runs down my lower back until it settles just low enough to where his fingers rest on the top of my ass. His other hand is in my own as he leads us around to the song.

I'm surprised that I can suddenly keep up without tripping over myself.

"Just needed the right man to take the lead." His growly voice hits me right in the chest.

"And you're that man?" I ask, raising an eyebrow. I am desperately trying to play it cool. The last thing I want is for him to think he has any kind of upper hand here. It'll just go straight to his damn ego.

"You tell me, poppyseed. Am I?"

I bite my lower lip and look away from his gaze. I can't handle it; it's too intense.

"I'm going to get whiplash, Rhett Black."

He grunts.

"Back to not speaking, I see." I'm complaining, whining like the child he makes me out to be. And that pisses me off even more than his grunts do. "You're a pain in my ass, do you know that? Yelling at me, then leaning in to kiss me. Yelling at me, then sticking your thumb in my mouth. Now you're yelling at other men and telling me I should only be dancing with and touching you, only for you to go all silent on me!"

If people had stopped looking at us, I had definitely just garnered the attention of the ones around us again. Because that rant seemed to get louder as I kept going. But I refuse to back down. I'm tired of getting treated like shit, only for him to shut himself down again.

"If you're going to put some sort of weird posses-sive caveman claim on me," I say, grinding the words out so I don't yell, "you damn well better be ready to follow through."

He looks down at me, his nostrils flared as he breathes heavily, trying to contain whatever emotion I just set off inside of him.

"You want me to follow through, Poppy?" he asks, that gravel voice turning into a growl.

I swallow. Do I?

"Yes," I breathe.

He chuckles darkly.

"Alright, then. Just remember, you asked for it."

And then he's tugging me toward the back door.

CHAPTER EIGHTEEN

Rhett

I YANK her across the dance floor and through the crowd of people. I can't wait any longer. I need to know what that mouth feels like against my own. But I refuse to have our first kiss happen with an audience. I want it quiet so that I can hear all her little moans I know she's going to give me.

When I push open the back door, the chill of the night air wraps around us. There's no one out here, but I round the corner just in case anyone else decides to come out here to smoke or something. And the second we're out of the line of sight, I push her against the wood siding. My thigh slips between hers, and my girl settles there like she's desperate for that little bit of pressure.

"I'm going to kiss you now," I tell her as my hands wrap around her neck and then weave into the short strands of her hair. I tug, and her mouth drops open just enough that her pink tongue can come out and lick the plump bottom lip.

God, she's gorgeous. Since coming here, her skin has broken out with a million freckles, and they're dotted all over her nose, cheeks, and forehead. And her eyes are a gorgeous honey-green color, even in the low light we're in now. They draw me in like a moth to a flame.

"Follow through, then, Rhett."

Her voice is husky and filled with desire. My cock twitches and begs to come to life as her soft body rubs against my own.

Finally, I lean over her and hover over her lips. Her eyes close, and she lifts her chin just slightly up toward me. She's begging for it, and I'm tired of holding back. I'm ready to follow through and give her exactly what she wants.

Our lips meet, softly at first. They're pillowy soft, and when she parts them for me, my tongue sweeps in and claims her. She tastes just as sweet as she smells, and my cock hardens. Her hips roll against me, rubbing her sweet jean-covered pussy on my thigh. And now all I can think about is how I could make her come, right here, right now. I could have that piece of her. And surely, that would tide me over.

If I could just hear her moan out my name, that would get me through the night.

Her hands grab hold of my shirt, fisting in the fabric as they tug me closer. Our mouths move against each other more insistently. Our teeth clash together, and I swallow her little sighs and moans with each swipe of my tongue. I devour her, fucking her mouth just like I want to fuck her cunt.

"Poppy," I groan as I pull back just slightly. Her lips are wet and swollen, and her eyes are heavy with lust as she looks up at me. Those pupils are blown wide, and her fingers run through the scruff on my jaw. "I'm gonna make you come now."

Her eyes widen in surprise, like all she expected was a little kiss. God, she has no idea what she has awoken inside of me.

"We're in public." Her voice is barely above a whisper.

I just grin and pull her back to me for another kiss.

"That won't stop me from making you shout my name as you come, poppyseed."

I grab hold of the front of her jeans, pulling them even tighter against her so that all the pressure is on her clit. She gasps, and her head falls forward to my chest.

"Oh, my god."

"You're going to grind that sweet little pussy on my thigh until you come shoutin' out my name. Okay, Poppy?"

When she looks up at me, her face and neck have

turned bright red. For someone with so much attitude, she sure is embarrassed easily.

I tug on her jeans again.

"Answer me."

"Okay. Yes. Okay."

Her hips begin to roll, stroking her pussy against the hard seam of her jeans and down onto the muscle of my thigh. Her hands are on my shoulders, and she's hanging her head as she pants and whimpers. My girl loves this, out in the open, taking her pleasure where anyone could come out and see.

There's only one issue — she isn't looking at me. And I need her full attention.

"Hey," I say, grabbing her jaw with my free hand. "Eyes on me."

"Rhett, I can't." She lets out a breathy laugh. "It's too much. I'm too embarrassed to just stare at you while I try to come."

"Too bad. Fight through it. You asked for me to follow through, this is me following through. If you don't like it, Poppy, you're free to hop off my leg and find someone else to get off with."

"No, don't make me leave. I want you, Rhett. Just you."

"Good girl."

I lean forward and kiss her cheek, then the side of her mouth, and then claim those lips as her hips pick up speed. She's close. Her breathing is erratic, and those sweet fucking moans are getting louder. I eat everything up like it's my last meal. I wish I could taste her. I wish it was my mouth making her come, but this is going to be good enough for now.

"Oh, god," she moans, pulling away from my kiss so she can get a deep breath.

But she behaves, keeping her eyes on me and fighting through whatever embarrassment she has. I have no idea what she could be self-conscious about. Everything about her is fucking breathtaking. From her eyes to her breasts to her stomach and hips, all the way down to her cute, pink-painted toes. I want to devour her.

"Are you going to come for me, Poppy?" My mouth is close to her ear as I kiss the pulse point on her throat. It hammers against my lips as I nibble and lick and suck.

"Yes. Rhett, please."

I pull even tighter on her jeans, stretching them to the point I'm worried I might rip them. That's not something I want to have to explain to my brothers. But they hold, and her hips give a few more thrusts against my thigh before she's shouting my name out into the empty field next to the bar. It's the sweetest fucking sound I think I've ever heard.

Her hands slide down my arms and rest on my biceps as her body slumps back against the wall. I let go of her jeans, only to unbutton and unzip them, quickly shoving my hand inside before she realizes what's happening. Her eyes grow wide when my fingers find her slick slit and tease her clit.

"What are you doing?"She looks around, breathless and panting. Now that the high from her orgasm has passed, her eyes scan our surroundings as if she's worried someone will come out here and find us.

"Getting a taste." I slip a single finger inside of her, curling it just enough to press firmly on that spot deep within. Christ, she is wet and tight and so fucking warm. It's going to be heaven when I slide inside of her later tonight. She moans, and then I'm slipping out, bringing that finger in between us.

"See that, poppyseed? What a mess… See what I do to you?"

She nods, and then I lick her juices from my skin. Her scent and taste cause a growl to slip from my chest.

"Oh, okay." She watches me, licking her lips as I suck the last bit from my finger. "That was insanely hot."

I grin. "It's taking saint-level restraint not to rip this denim from your gorgeous thighs and bury my tongue so far into your cunt you feel me for days."

"Jesus Christ." She exhales.

"How was that for following through?" I ask her, fastening her jeans back in place.

She clears her throat. "Yeah, for sure. Good. Good job."

That gets a laugh from me. A real, genuine laugh.

"How about I show you what a good job I can do when there's a bed involved?"

She makes a little noise, swallowing back her nervousness.

"Now? How do we get home?"

Shit. Good point. I didn't drive. I run my hand through my hair and then realize I've done this enough for my brothers; they can do this for me. They'll be fine to get a ride with someone in town. Someone in there is bound to be drivin' out our way.

"Go up front to Hayes' truck. I'll meet you up there in a sec, okay?"

"Okay."

I smack her ass, and it finally brings back some of that Poppy sass I'm used to. She whips around and points a finger in my direction.

"Careful, cowboy. Don't bite off more than you can chew."

"Oh, poppyseed. I very much intend to take a bite."

CHAPTER NINETEEN

Poppy

I HAVE a few thoughts buzzing through my mind. One: my panties are wet and uncomfortable. Two: does that count as someone else giving me an orgasm? Because technically, I did most of the work, but if it does count, Rhett has officially broken my streak. And three: what the fuck am I doing?

I lean back against the passenger side door of Hayes' work truck. I'm trying to regulate my breathing, but holy shit, Rhett has turned my night on its head. Thank god I didn't have time to drink. I want to be fully sober for what's about to happen because if he can make me come up against the wall of a bar, I'm excited to see what he can do when we're in private.

The front door of the bar opens, and I push off the truck to watch him walk over to me. God, he's hand-some. Whatever he did with his hair this evening is ruined now from my hands running through it earlier. His form is a force to be reckoned with as his heavy boots crunch on the gravel.

He dangles the keys as he gets closer. I try not to let my excitement show. Play it cool, Poppy. Play it cool.

"They'll get a ride home with someone from the bar," he says, closing in on me as he forces my back against the truck door again. "And now I get to have you all to myself for the rest of the night."

He kisses me again, devouring me from the inside out with his tongue. His hands are in my hair, and his body is pressed against my own. I could die happy. I've never been with an older man, let alone a cowboy. I can tell the difference even just in the way he kisses me, like he possesses me. Like I'm *his*.

He breaks the kiss and looks down at me, smirking when I struggle to open my eyes and look at him. He's kissed me fucking senseless. What does he expect?

"Ready to go home, Poppy?"

I nod. "Yes, please."

Reaching behind me, he nudges me out of the way to open the door. Before I can climb in myself, he's picking me up at the waist and setting me inside. He didn't even have to squat and lift with his knees. That man literally just used pure arm strength to lift my over-two-hundred-pound ass into the damn truck.

Getting my ass thrown around in the bedroom is looking very promising.

———————————◆

The drive home is painfully quiet. But it honestly does nothing to dampen the mood. Instead, it makes the anticipation all that stronger. It's like we're both on edge to get home, ready to get naked in bed together. The energy between us is fucking thrumming the entire way back to the ranch.

We pull into the driveway, and he turns the lights off as we go down the long dirt road. The main house is barely in sight when he pulls off on the side to park. The truck bobs and weaves in and out of the ditch and then halts as he puts it in park.

"Don't wanna alert anyone we're home this early," he says, sensing my questions. "The kids would be on us like stink on a pig."

I snort. Gross simile, but he's not wrong.

"Makes sense." I take a deep breath, nervous all over again. Once we get out of this truck, there's no going back. "Yours or mine?" I ask, looking over at him.

He smirks. "I don't trust my momma to not bring those kids over first thing in the morning just to mess with me after a night of drinkin'. It'll have to be yours tonight, poppyseed."

Tonight. He says that like he plans for there to be

more nights, and maybe some of those nights, I'll be going to his. How will his kids handle that? Am I ready for that? Is this going to be a relationship? Jesus Christ, Poppy. You barely know the guy, and you're already thinking about relationships.

"You are thinking awful loud over there," he murmurs, reaching over to run the back of his fingers over my cheek. "Wanna let me into that brain?"

"God, no." I laugh. "You don't need to be privy to all my dirty thoughts about you, Rhett Black."

He turns, quickly opening the door and jumping out. I watch him as he walks around the hood and then opens my door. He stares at me, caging me in the truck with his arms as he does so.

"Poppy," he starts. "I have been fighting whatever the hell this is since I saw those strawberries on your underwear that first day. And that mouth you have on you…" He trails off and stares at my mouth.

"My mouth?"

"Mm," he hums. "The way you bite back, sticking up for yourself and puttin' me in my place." He drags his thumb across my lips. "I'd like to see how pretty it looks wrapped around my cock."

"Oh" is all I can think of to say. But I'm thinking I would like that as well.

"So get your ass out of that truck, and let me take you home."

I do not have to be told twice. Sliding out of the

seat, I let our bodies brush against each other on my way down. His eyes darken when I bite my lip.

"Let's go, then, cowboy."

The walk over to my little house is a quick one. We both practically run across the fields to get to it, and I'm shocked I don't break an ankle on the way with the way he's tugging on me. A man on a mission, it seems. Not that I mind. I can't remember the last time a man was this excited to get me undressed.

"I left it unlocked," I tell him as we walk up the steps of the front porch.

He throws open the screen door and then pushes the front door so hard I'm afraid he's going to take it off its hinges. It bounces off the wall behind it, and I help it close before he breaks it. When I turn back around, he's staring at the wine stain on the rug with a big smile on his face.

"I'll get a new one in here," he says, looking up at me as he toes off his boots.

"I don't care about the damn rug, Rhett."

"No?" He stalks toward me, slow and measured steps. I kick off my own shoes, shifting me down a few inches so I have to really crane my neck to look up at him.

"No." I sink to my knees and unbutton his jeans, never taking my eyes off his. They heat as he watches me tug his jeans down over his hips and thighs. Breaking eye contact, I take in the thick outline of him behind the tight black boxers he has on. There's a wet spot at the band where precum has leaked from his tip.

I did that.

"Take it out."

My eyes dart up at his commanding voice, but I quickly tuck my fingers under the band of his boxers and pull them down, letting his cock free of the restraint. It bobs forward and stands straight out toward me, begging for my mouth. He steps back to kick the clothing off, and I watch as he tugs his shirt from his torso. He does that superhot thing where they grab it from the back and pull it over their head.

Swoon. This man knows what he's doing. And when his body is finally fully naked for me, I grow even wetter between my thighs. He's built from fucking stone with hair dusted across his chest and stomach. His hips are cut into sharp angles that point directly where my pussy wants me to be. And that cock. My god, that cock.

I'm a little worried it's going to split me in half. It's like the four-wheeler experience all over again. Except this time, I have full confidence this man is going to get me to the finish line…multiple times.

And then that same growly voice commands me again.

"Show me what that pretty mouth looks like wrapped around my cock, baby."

CHAPTER TWENTY

Poppy

I TAKE the head into my mouth, tasting the salty fluid that has gathered there. Rhett's eyes roll to the back of his head as I begin to work him over, using both of my hands to help me get going. As I take him deeper and deeper into my throat, I'm thankful I'm one of the lucky ones who were born with barely any gag reflex. It's definitely coming in handy here.

His hands sink into my hair and grab as much as they can, pulling tightly enough that my eyes begin to water. My hands are everywhere all at once, on his cock and palming his balls, then down the strong muscles of his thighs, only to move around to his ass where I can pull him deeper into me.

His moans urge me on. I swear they turn me into a woman possessed. I'm desperate to hear more, so I touch and suck and lick everything that might elicit more. I stroke him from root to tip as I lick and suck one of his balls into my mouth. This makes him roll up onto the balls of his feet, and I'm pretty proud of myself for making a man's toes literally curl.

"Yes, baby," he praises. "My little slut knows just how to suck my cock, doesn't she?"

God, the mouth on this man. I glance up at him and nod like the good fucking girl I am and then take the other one into my mouth. I roll it slowly with my tongue and suck until it pops out and makes him hiss through his teeth.

I wonder how long it's been for him. He's a grumpy asshole who has two kids; I can't imagine him getting the time to sleep around a whole lot. Even the thought of him being with someone else has jealousy burning a hole through my stomach lining.

"That's it, Poppy," he growls as he begins to really fuck my face. He must be close because his hips are moving erratically, like he can't hold back any longer. When I look up at him and relax my throat, I'm rewarded with the sexiest growl I think I've ever heard.

Christ, this man.

I try to breathe through my nose, moaning when I can to make it vibrate against him. He grits his teeth and flexes his ass against my hands. He's so close, and I'm desperate for it. I need to taste him.

"I'm going to come in that tight little throat, Poppy.

Be a good girl and swallow it for me, yeah? Swallow every drop I give you."

I can't say anything, so I just give over to him, staring up at him as he ruthlessly fucks my face. I'm not sure what it says about me, but I am soaked. Nothing has ever turned me on the way Rhett losing control does. I'm even grinding my hips when I can to get some kind of relief against my jeans.

He raises up on his toes again, and I feel him swell and release. I swallow over and over again, determined not to miss a drop. My throat constricts around his sensitive head, dragging more groans from his chest. His mouth falls open, and his eyes squeeze shut as he finishes.

"Fuck," he grunts, pulling me off him.

I lick my sore lips and then smirk up at him. I'm unable to help myself. I *have* to push his damn buttons.

"That was quick."

"Woman." He urges me up onto my feet, never letting go of the back of my head. I love it when he calls me woman. "You just sucked the soul from my damn body. Don't start."

I laugh, but he swallows it with a kiss, sweeping his tongue inside my mouth to taste himself. His hands work on tugging my top out of the front of my jeans and then over my head. I lift my arms and let him get a good look at my boring T-shirt bra. Had I known we were going to be fooling around, I would've dressed for it.

My jeans are next, and he makes quick work of them like he did at the bar, popping the button and tugging down the zipper before pushing them down my thighs. I wiggle the rest of the way out of them and kick them off to the side. Even my underwear is a boring black cotton. He must be thrilled.

"You're fucking beautiful, do you know that?"

I can feel myself blush, but I refuse to look away. I'm not going to act like some embarrassed little thing that can't even stand half-naked in front of a handsome, ripped man.

"And you," I tell him, running my hands over his chest, shoulders, and down his biceps, "have a farmer's tan."

He bursts out laughing, his head dropping back. I can't help but laugh along with him. It's broken some of the embarrassment I felt.

"Come here," he says, wrapping his arms around my body. I let him lift me up, and I wrap my legs around his waist as he kisses me.

"Bedroom," I say against his mouth.

"Yes, ma'am."

There's an anxious excitement brewing in my stomach. Like I said, a man this handsome gets a girl's hopes up. And my hopes are way, way up. I want to know how good he is with his tongue and his fingers. I'm a little hesitant about the cock that's pressing against my panties, but I look forward to it nonetheless.

Once we get to the bedroom, he tosses me down on the bed, making me bounce before righting myself. He stands there and stares at me, his naked form looking fucking godly at the foot of the bed.

"I don't want to feed into your ego, Rhett Black," I tell him, bending my knees and spreading my legs. His eyes dip to the apex of my thighs. "But you're pretty damn handsome."

He smirks. "I won't let it go to my head, poppyseed. Promise."

He leans forward on his hands and crawls onto the bed between my legs. His lips softly touch my knee and then move down the inside of my thigh. When he gets to my pussy, he moves, starting at the other knee. It's driving me crazy, the waiting and teasing.

"Tell me what you like, Poppy."

My heart hammers through my chest as I watch him hover over my center. He presses an open-mouthed kiss over my underwear and lays his tongue flat against my clit. The sensation is enough to make my hips buck into his face.

"I—" I start but realize I'm not actually sure. Seeing as no one has ever managed to get me there, I'm not sure what I actually like a partner to do.

"Use your words, Poppy," he teases before dipping back down between my thighs.

Christ, that feels amazing.

"I don't know exactly," I tell him honestly. When he

looks up at me, an eyebrow raised like he doesn't believe me, I decide to just spill my guts.

"No one has ever managed to, ya know, get me there," I tell him, my mouth moving faster than my brain is. "I'm not saying I've never had an orgasm. Trust me, I have. I own a rose toy that makes me see stars on a regular basis. Well, not on a *too* regular basis. I'm not, like, addicted to porn or anything. Hell, I mostly read my porn."

I take a breath and soldier on. Word vomit. Word vomit everywhere.

"Anyway, what I'm saying is I've just never had a partner able to make me come. They always either give up too quickly or don't keep going when I fucking say *keep going*. They finish too early or just straight up have no clue what they're doing. Sometimes I wonder if I ruined myself with vibrators."

I laugh nervously.

"But that can't be the case, right? Because I came earlier with you at the bar, so clearly, I'm capable. You know, there was this one time when an ex had my hips propped up on a pillow, and he was hitting this amazing spot. I swear, I was so close. But then he told me that it felt too good and he couldn't hold on. Three seconds later, everything was over, and I was left horny and unsatisfied."

Rhett's hand comes down and closes over my mouth, effectively shutting off my nervous rant. My cheeks heat, and I pray that the mattress below us will swallow me whole. What the fuck was I doing?

"First things first, Poppy Sharpe." His voice is all rough gravel as his fingers tighten on my cheeks. He leans over me, his eyes holding mine captive. My pussy is soaked. "I never want to hear you speak about another man while in bed with me. Do you understand?"

I nod.

"Good. Good girl." He kisses my nose. "And second, anyone you were with before was a boy. You're with me now, and I'm a man who doesn't leave his woman wanting. I will eat that pretty little pussy of yours for hours if that's what it takes. I will let you ride my cock any way you like until you're screaming my name so loud the windows rattle. Your pleasure comes first, no matter what. So don't you dare fake it with me. We're here 'til you soak these sheets. Got that?"

"Oh, fuck," I whimper against the palm of his hand. He smiles, and it is filled with confidence.

"Oh, fuck is right, baby. Now, spread those thick thighs for me, and let me lick you until you scream."

CHAPTER TWENTY-ONE

Poppy

MY PANTIES GET TUGGED down my body, and I lie back flat and try to relax. There are so many butterflies swarming in my stomach that it's hard to just give myself over to what he's doing.

When he pushes my thighs farther apart, the cool air skates across my pussy and makes my back arch. I'm throbbing for him, my clit swollen and needy. I can feel how wet I am as he uses his thumbs to spread me wide.

"Look at you," he says, his voice deep and full of wonder. "So pink and wet. Is this all for me, Poppy?"

I nod.

He blows cool air against my heated flesh, forcing a whimper from my throat.

"Say it. I need to hear you say it. Is this pussy all for me?"

"Yes, Rhett."

"And only me?"

I struggle to find my voice because him claiming me like this has my chest aching, and I don't even know why. It's just sex, Poppy. It's just dirty talk. That's all it is.

"Only you." I reach down and grab a fistful of his hair, making him finally look up at my face. "Now, stop fucking around, make good on your promise, and eat my *pretty little pussy*."

He chuckles. "Anything for you, poppyseed."

His mouth descends on my clit, and he sucks it into his mouth with so much force my toes curl and my hips jump off the bed. He wraps his strong arms around my waist to ground me and begins his assault all over again. This man sucks and licks and bites in all the right places.

"That!" I almost shout when he teases my clit with the tip of his tongue while he sucks on as much of my pussy as he can fit in his damn mouth. It's overwhelming and so fucking delicious. "That right there!"

He doesn't lift his head to say anything or to smile or brag. He. Keeps. Going. And then to push me even closer to the edge, he uses a finger or a knuckle, I don't know which, to circle my entrance. It teases the nerves there, and along with the consistent motion on my clit, I'm already close to finishing.

Holy shit, this man makes it look easy.

"Rhett," I moan, squeezing his head with my thighs

and tugging hard on the soft strands of his hair. I've never been with a man with such nice hair, and I soak it up, running my fingers through it like I'll never get enough.

He moans against me, skyrocketing my pleasure. Knowing that he's enjoying this almost as much as I am has my whole body heated. The sensation starts deep in my belly and spreads up my spine and down to my toes. I fight against his hold on my waist to push myself closer to that sweet, sinful mouth of his.

"I'm going to come," I pant. He doesn't change anything about what he's doing. His jaw must be aching from the constant motion, but he doesn't stop.

"Rhett!" I shout his name as my back arches and my breath stalls. My pussy clenches and begs for him to fill me as the orgasm sweeps through my body. His tongue sees me through it, only letting up when my breathing starts to return to normal. With long, slow licks, he tastes every bit of me. He bites on my lips and then dips his tongue deep inside to taste what he did to me.

"That was way too easy," he says, leaving a trail of wet kisses up my stomach and over the swells of my breasts. His beard and mouth are wet from my juices, but I don't care. I'm floating on cloud nine, and I want a fucking taste of what he did to me. I tug him forward and kiss him senseless.

Reaching between us, I grab his hard cock and

stroke him until he breaks the kiss. His forehead drops to mine as he pants.

"I didn't expect…" he says, trailing off as he tries to find the right words. "I didn't come prepared. I don't have a condom." His hips push forward as I squeeze him at the base.

I look up at him, holding his gaze.

"I'm on birth control."

He sighs, and his eyes close.

"I don't—" He grunts when my wrist twists just the right way. "I don't want to take advantage of you, and I know it's too late now, but I'm clean. I haven't been with anyone since before Wade was born."

My heart stutters. I am far too happy to hear that.

"I'm clean, too. I always use a condom."

He raises an eyebrow, probably wondering why I don't have any on me if I always use one..

"What? I didn't bring condoms to the middle of fucking nowhere Montana. I wasn't planning on getting laid."

He groans. "Which is exactly why we shouldn't be doing this. You didn't come here to get tangled up in a single dad."

"I may not have come here with the intention, Rhett Black," I say, grabbing his jaw so that he's forced to look at me, "but I wouldn't have it any other way."

His eyes bob back and forth between my own.

"Now, shove this monster cock inside of me and show me how a real man fucks his woman."

"Christ, Poppy. You got quite the mouth on you."

He kisses me, bruising my lips with the effort as I run the head of his cock up and down my slit. Just when I think he's about to push inside of me, he pulls away, sitting back on his heels between my thighs.

"Take off your bra."

This man *never* has to tell me twice. I reach behind my back and unsnap the clasp before tugging it away from my body and tossing it on the floor. He palms my breasts and rolls my hard nipples between his fingers. I've never been big on nipple play, but my body is so keyed up on this man that anywhere he touches feels like it has a direct line to my clit.

His calloused hands tickle as they run over my waist and belly, causing goose bumps to break out across my entire body. I love my body, but sometimes when men touch my stomach, I get self-conscious or worry that they're fetishizing my curves. But when Rhett does it? The way he looks at me settles any nerves I may have had. Because he looks at me like I was put on this Earth just for him.

When he gets to my hips, he tugs me down and then lifts my ass up on his thighs. Taking hold of his cock, he taps it against my clit a few times, sending little shocks of electricity deep into my core.

"I want to watch as I sink inside you inch by inch,"

he says, staring at where he's pushing inside of me. "I'm going to stretch you so good, poppyseed. I can't wait to feel you come all over my cock. And then I'm gonna fill you up and watch as my cum leaks out of this tight cunt."

Jesus. Fucking. Christ.

CHAPTER TWENTY-TWO

Rhett

I SINK INSIDE of her slowly, relishing every second of the way her pussy stretches to accommodate me. I'm not average-size, and it does take me a second to work my way in. I don't want to hurt her.

She props herself up on her elbows, and even though her eyebrows are drawn together, she watches us come together with lust in her eyes. And when I'm finally all the way in, her head drops back, exposing the long column of her throat.

God, she's gorgeous. There's a sheen of sweat on her skin, and her pale pink nipples are pebbled and begging to be sucked. I lean forward, taking one in my mouth to make her moan and run her hands through my hair again. I love it when she does that. It's a sweet gesture that turns rough when she's in the throes of it.

"God, you take me so well, Poppy." I like the way she lights up a little each time I praise her.

"You're so big," she groans. "I feel like I'm being split in two!"

I laugh and kiss her collarbone. "So dramatic."

Her fingers tighten on my hair to punish me.

"I am not dramatic." She tugs me to her face and kisses me. She kisses like she speaks, fighting me every step of the way like our tongues are in a war zone.

Her hips begin to rotate as she grinds herself down onto my shaft. She is tight and wet, and I cannot take much more of that before I come. So I take control, digging my fingers into her soft hips as I pull out and thrust back in. A deep moan comes from her chest as she grabs onto my hands.

"I'm not gonna last long, Poppy," I admit. "Because this pussy was made for me, and it's been a long time since I've been with a woman. So I need you to be a good girl and let this body of yours enjoy the ride. I refuse to finish before I get one more orgasm from you."

I move slowly at first, letting her body get used to how I'm going to fuck her. Before the night is over, I plan to fuck this pussy so hard she'll feel me for days. Her hands go to her nipples, those delicate fingers tweaking and tugging on them while her hips lift to meet every thrust I give her. The sounds of our sex echo through the quiet bedroom.

"Touch yourself, Poppy." She stops what she's doing

and bites her lip, looking up at me like she's suddenly shy again. "None of that, baby. Show me what you like. Show me how you touch yourself."

"I will if you stop holding back," she tells me, letting one of her hands drift south across her belly. "I can tell you're trying to be gentle when all you really want to do is let go and fuck me into this mattress."

The second she touches her clit, I lose any and all ability to hold back. I watch as she rolls her clit between her fingers the best she can while I plow into her ruthlessly. Every few strokes, her fingers slip in between us to toy with the base of my cock, giving me the extra sensation I didn't need when trying *not* to come.

"Tell me you're close, poppyseed." Her eyes are shut, and I watch her tits bounce with each thrust as she concentrates on her pleasure.

"So fucking close," she moans.

"Don't you dare lie to me, Poppy Sharpe. No faking it!"

"Shut the fuck up and let me come, you insufferable ass!"

She screams as her orgasm rips through her, forcing her pussy to clench around me like a goddamn vise grip. I can barely fit inside of her while the pretty thing pulses around me. But that's all it takes to trigger my own release, and with one more deep thrust, I'm emptying myself inside of her.

"Poppy!" I shout her name and then bury my face in

the crook of her neck as all of my muscles seize up with pleasure. Jesus Christ, I'm seeing stars.

Her legs wrap around me, and her arms tug me down to her torso. I collapse and blink away the floaters in my vision. We're both breathin' heavily, and then she starts laughing. She is fucking laughing.

"I just fucked my boss."

She snorts and starts laughing even harder. When I pull back to look at her, she slaps her hand across her mouth as tears start to leak from the sides of her eyes.

"I'm sorry, I'm sorry," she says, waving away my concern as she tries to gather herself. "It's just...you were *such* an asshole, Rhett."

I grin and roll off her.

"Would an asshole get a warm cloth to clean you up?"

She just giggles as me and my bare ass walk to the bathroom across the hall and get something to clean her up. She's settled by the time I get back, and shit if my cum leaking out of her isn't the sexiest sight in the world. Her sex is swollen, and I know for sure she's going to be feeling it tomorrow morning.

Luckily, she has the day off, so I can force her to rest.

"You know how good this pussy looks with my cum inside it, Poppy?"

Her cheeks flush, and she licks that plump bottom lip.

"Your mouth…"

I just smile and finish cleaning her up, tossing the rag to somewhere behind me before climbing back up on the bed. Pulling the covers back, I help her get under them and then tug her into my body.

"Can you open that window?" she asks, gesturin' to the one above the headboard. "I like the fresh air."

Shoving the thing open, I take comfort in the smells of the ranch after sunset. It's more crisp, fresher than what you get when you're shoveling shit all day. She turns around in my arms and buries her head into my chest. She fits too perfectly in my arms. She smells too fucking good. This is too fucking comfortable.

"I know we should probably talk about what the hell this means." She yawns and wraps a leg around my hip. She molds to me like she was meant to fit in this spot. "But can it wait 'til tomorrow? Because I am exhausted."

She's right. I probably fucked up big time tonight. But it had been so long since I was tempted by a woman other than my ex-wife. Not that I'm still hung up on her, but I just knew I couldn't go sleepin' around with any woman who looked my way. And there have been plenty. But I have the kids now, and they come first. Always.

But Poppy blew into my damn ranch like a wildfire, burnin' me up and my defenses down. Since the moment I saw her, something clicked inside of me. Shit, that sounds corny as hell. And it still doesn't excuse what I've done. Because now we have to navigate whatever the hell this is while also keeping up our damn working relationship.

And there's the kids. And my parents. And my brothers…who are never going to let me live this shit down.

I hold in a sigh. I don't need her to worry about all the thoughts fightin' around in my head right now.

I kiss the top of her head and then realize that little bun is still intact. Gently, I work the hairband out of her wavy hair, careful not to pull like Joey says I always do. And after it's out, I rub the crown of her scalp. I know Joey's always gets sore after wearin' her hair up all day.

She moans. "Shit, that feels good."

"Go to sleep, Poppy."

"Bossy."

"You called me an insufferable ass and then laughed at me right after I came. I think I'm allowed to be a little bossy."

She grunts.

"That's my thing," I tell her. "The grunting."

That gets another laugh out of her.

"Shut up, cowboy."

I do, and I count the seconds until she's snoring softly. Only then do I let myself close my eyes and relax enough to fall asleep with her in my arms.

CHAPTER
TWENTY-THREE

Poppy

I STARTLE AWAKE, sitting up like a vampire in an old movie but with serious force. And for some odd reason, Rhett is leaning over me, which means our heads collide really, really fucking hard.

"God dammit, woman!" he growls.

"Motherfucking shit balls!" I shout. "Rhett! What the hell?"

His hand comes around my mouth, effectively shutting me up as I rub the pounding pain in my forehead. His eyes are wide and grumpy. He looks very, very grumpy. I raise an eyebrow, but then I hear it. Someone is knocking on my front door. I swat his hand away.

"Who is it?" I whisper.

"Poppy?" Katherine. It's his mom. His mom is standing on my front porch, and I have her son naked in my bed.

"Oh, shit." I try not to burst out laughing at the look on his face. He is fucking terrified.

"Poppy! We brought you breakfast!"

Now it's my fucking turn to be terrified. Because that was Jolene's sweet voice. My eyes go wide, and he nods his head.

"Yeah, you have to go answer your damn door." Growly ass this morning.

"Dramatic," I say with a sigh. "Put your clothes on, and sneak out the back or something."

"What am I? Sixteen?"

"You're sure as shit acting like it." I throw a robe over myself. "Coming, sorry! One sec!" I shout toward the door.

"My shit is in the living room."

"Oh, that is unfortunate for you."

"Poppy," he growls.

I roll my eyes. "I'll throw 'em down the hall. Get dressed and sneak out the back or hide in my room. But I can guarantee they'll be coming inside."

"You have me fit to be fuckin' tied, woman."

His hair is sticking up all over his head, and even his beard has a bit of bed head. Even when he's grumpy, I can't help but get a little gooey-eyed over him. The sun is coming in through the window above the bed, and it's shining on his tanned shoulders. My eyes roam over the hair on his chest and stomach… I've never been with anyone so hairy. I really, really like it.

"Quit gawkin' and go answer the damn door."

"God, you're grumpy in the mornings."

He stands up and stalks over toward me, backing me against the wall. God, he smells good. His hands cup my jaw, and when he leans in, I feel myself go up on my tiptoes, trying to get closer to his mouth. I want him to kiss me. I want him to still want me in the light of day.

"And you, Poppy Sharpe, are still dripping with my cum. So go out there and get rid of them so we can take a shower."

Did he just say *we*?

I groan and savor the softness of his lips as they skate over my own.

"Where is she?" I hear Wade ask.

Both Rhett and I laugh.

"I should probably go out there."

"Probably," he says, kissing me again. And when I walk out of my room, he slaps me hard on my ass, making me yelp. I think seriously about keeping his clothes from him but decide just in case they do see him, it's probably better if he has clothes on.

Jolene spots me when I walk out into the living room. Her little face is pushed up against one of the living room windows with her hands around her eyes. I wave at her and then lean over to pick up all of Rhett's shit when she runs back to the door. He reaches out into the hallway and grabs his clothes right before I open the door.

"Hi, guys!" They both fight to get their arms around me like they haven't seen me in days.

"We brought you breakfast because our uncles always wake up Sunday mornin's starving," Wade tells me.

"Daddy says it's because they drink like fish. But I don't think fish drink." Jolene hands me a plate piled high with biscuits and eggs and bacon. My stomach growls aggressively.

"Sorry it's so early," Katherine says, still standing in the doorway. "We were getting everything ready to make the rounds to the boys' houses when these two thought you'd want some breakfast, too, since you went out with everyone. And you know me, I can't help but feed every mouth in sight."

"Thank you so much for thinking of me." When I look up from the kids, I notice her eyes straying to the floor...where next to the big-ass stain of wine...are Rhett's motherfucking cowboy boots.

Her cheeks turn pink, and I can tell she's biting back a smile.

"*Very* sorry to intrude," she says again, looking at me with a sly smile. *Shit*. Rhett is gonna kill me. "Guys, let's go. Let Poppy eat her breakfast in peace. It's her day off today."

"But we want to hang out with her!" Jolene pouts.

"How about y'all come see me tomorrow for lunch? I heard we're getting some new animals delivered.

Maybe we can convince your uncle Wells to take us to see them?"

"Yes!" Wade lunges and shoves his fist into the air like he's won the lottery.

"Okay, let's go!" Katherine tries her best to get them moving, but it's like herding cats when it comes to kids.

"We're going to Daddy's next?" Jolene asks.

Katherine's eyes shoot to mine, and I shake my head as discreetly as possible. She needs to give him a bit of a head start if he's going to make it over to his before the kids do.

"Let's do your uncles first. That way, I can just drop y'all at your daddy's when we get there."

I mouth her a thank-you, and she just nods and smiles. I don't know what I was expecting as a reaction once she saw the boots, but there was a tight nervousness in my stomach. I'm a lot younger than him, and I'm his freaking employee. She totally would've been within her rights to fire me on the spot.

But that's not Katherine. That's not his family.

The door shuts behind them, and I go over to the little island in my kitchen and hop up onto the barstool, wincing at the soreness between my legs. As I peel back the plastic wrap, the delicious scent of homemade food fills my soul with joy. I could get used to this. House calls with amazing food, family dinners, and a hard day's work that leaves you the best kind of exhausted at the end.

I never want to leave.

"That was close," Rhett says, walking up behind me to wrap his arms around my shoulders. I lean back into his warmth.

"Well, maybe a little too close, considering your momma saw your boots by the door."

"Shit." He pulls away. "I was hopin' I had pushed them far enough out of the way."

"Oh, well." I shrug, spinning around to watch him sit on the couch and tug them on. "She didn't seem to care. In fact, she was biting back a smile like it was the funniest thing in the world."

He rolls his eyes and grunts. "That sounds like Momma."

"You're grumpy today."

He sighs and rests his elbows on his thighs. His head hangs down, and I start to get a little kernel of worry blooming in my stomach. I didn't want this to be a one-night thing, and I definitely didn't want *him* to be the one to end it. Somehow, that makes it worse, like he pities me or something. Like I'm just some kid that can't handle whatever it is this is.

"I'm not grumpy," he finally says, standing and walking over to me. He leans against the island and tucks a stray lock of hair behind my ear. "Just a bit stressed, if I'm being honest."

"I do prefer honesty." I take a bite of bacon, and he reaches across me to grab a biscuit. I slap his hand away. "No, sir. You have your own breakfast coming. You can leave mine alone."

He laughs and kisses me. "Talk later?"

I look into his dark honey eyes and decide I'm willing to hold off on talking about what's happening, seeing as his kids are going to be at his house any minute. We have more to think about than just us. There are more people involved.

I nod.

"Maybe you can sneak over sometime this week after the kids have gone to bed." He kisses the crook of my neck and slowly moves up until he takes the shell of my ear between his teeth.

"You'll have to learn to be quiet," I breathe.

He chuckles, his warm breath skating across my cheek before he kisses it.

"See you later, poppyseed."

I shamelessly watch him walk away, because his ass in those jeans is porn. Straight up cowboy porn. And it's getting logged into my brain for when he's an ass to me next and I need to remind myself why I let him get in my pants.

CHAPTER TWENTY-FOUR

Poppy

THE ANIMALS DIDN'T END up getting dropped off until later in the week because of a heat wave that's sweeping through the area. It slowed down a lot of shit that needed to be done on the ranch and put deliveries behind because of people all over struggling to get stuff done.

So now it's already Friday, and we're just now getting to integrate the new dogs. Meanwhile, the goats and chickens are being taken care of by Rhett and a few of the other guys that work for him. At least, that's what Wells has told me. I wouldn't know what Rhett is doing because I haven't heard from him since Sunday morning.

He's avoiding me like the plague. I go to Katherine's every morning, and every morning, she tells me he got an early start to avoid the heat. Wells and Hayes just roll their eyes and tell me he's "just being Rhett." Which does not make me feel any better.

I wasn't asking for a damn marriage proposal, but I certainly wasn't expecting to be ghosted. He promised we would talk. He suggested we'd be seeing each other. And yet, here we are.

"Heard from Rhett?" Hayes asks from where he's sitting. He's been coming over here all week, sitting with the dogs while he plays guitar for me and Wells.

"What do you think?"

I refuse to look at him because I know my emotions are all over my face. I feel stupid and embarrassed. Sweat is dripping down my back and into my eyes. I know my boob sweat is making puddles in my bra. Christ, even the backs of my knees are sweating. We have every fan going in this damn barn to keep it cool enough for the animals, but it's still hot when you add manual labor into the mix.

Wells told me they want to get it outfitted for temperature control in the summer. They've already got it set up for Montana winters to keep them warm, but it's rarely warm enough to warrant it in the summer. Lately, though, he says they've been getting random heat waves, and it's making everyone miserable.

Can confirm because I'm officially fucking miserable.

I look toward the barn door because I hear the kids' squeals of laughter floating in. It must be lunchtime.

Katherine hasn't missed a single day of coming up here with sandwiches and iced tea. It's still awkward as hell for me to be around her because I know she knows. But she hasn't brought it up once. We are just living with the elephant in the room, choosing to ignore it like a piece of very normal furniture.

Hayes jumps to his feet as she rounds the corner, trying to look busy.

"Saw that," she says, handing out the sandwiches while the kids go play with the puppies, who are growing like weeds.

"Thank you, Katherine." I smile at her, and she gives me a playful wink.

"The guys up at the horse barn need some help," she says, not really addressing anyone in particular. "Your daddy has gone up to help Rhett but wants someone else to come."

"I am not muckin' out stalls in this heat," Hayes says through a mouthful.

"Just for that, yes you are." Katherine gives him a look, and it only takes him a second to respond. Groaning, he tosses his guitar over his back and pouts the entire way out of the barn, shoving that sandwich in his mouth so fast I think he might choke.

"I'll go up in a minute," Wells says.

"Think we could stay with you?" I look down, and Jolene's warm brown eyes are looking back up at me. Her hair is in braided pigtails today, her baby hairs falling out and floating around her face. Her nose and cheeks are red from the sun.

"Of course you can. You can take the little ones outside for a few minutes if you want. They probably need to potty after their lunch." They're still so young and underweight that they're getting fed three times a day, with treats in between. They're going to be spoiled rotten.

Katherine helps get the puppies outside and then tells me to send the kids back the second I get tired of them. I could never get tired of these kids. They're incredibly well-behaved, if not a little ornery sometimes. But they have big hearts, and they're great with the dogs. It's a bit of a relief to have something to distract me from thoughts of Rhett.

Even if the distraction comes in the form of his kids.

"Keep forgetting to tell you," Wells says. "We have an adoption event happening in about a month."

"Oh, perfect! The puppies will be just the right age by then."

He nods. "I'm sure they'll go quick."

"That also puts it right around my birthday," I tell him. "The big two-seven."

"Oh, yeah? I'll have to tell Momma. She'll make you a big ole cake, and we'll all get drunk and make a big-ass bonfire."

"That sounds safe. Alcohol and fire."

He just rolls his eyes and laughs. "Don't be so dramatic. Hayes used to be a volunteer firefighter. He knows how to put somethin' out if it starts."

"Alright, alright. But we don't need to make a big deal out of it. It's just a birthday."

He clutches his hands over his heart like he's been wounded. "*Just* a birthday? Miss Poppy, there is no such thing on this ranch. Go big or go home."

"Uncle Wells! Wade is pissin' in the yard again!" Jolene's little voice comes in through the front doors.

"Daddy says I'm allowed to piss outside!" he shouts back.

"Only when there are no ladies present!"

"You're a *girl*."

"Poppy is right inside!"

I slap my hand over my mouth, trying not to laugh out loud.

"Okay, well, I guess I'll go handle *that*."

"Alright, I'm gonna let Betty out to eat on her long lead."

I let Wells handle that mess and go spend some time with Betty. Every day, I give her a little snack at lunchtime and open her door. She's started letting me get close enough to where I can put a long lead on her without snapping at me. So I tie her up to the wall on a twenty-foot lead and put a little snack in a bowl farther and farther away from her each day.

I'm desperate to get her to come out of her shell, and

I'm hoping once she sees that she can come out of her safe space and get rewarded for doing so, the next thing we can do is work on introducing her to other adults. Maybe even long walks outside to get her legs stretched. The farthest she goes now is outside to pee. And even that is a mountain to climb each time.

I move slowly inside her home, picking up her water bowl so I can clean it out and refill it. I speak softly to her, letting her know what I'm doing each step of the way, even though she has no clue what I'm saying. I hope it puts her a bit at ease.

I let the water hose run cold while I watch Wells and the kids play together in the grass. He's lying down, letting the puppies run all over him while Wade laughs and laughs like it's the funniest thing he's ever seen. Meanwhile, Jolene is pouting off to the side, just sitting cross-legged with one of the puppies on her lap. She's going to be heartbroken when that thing gets adopted. She has been joined at the hip with that specific one ever since she met them.

When the water is finally cold, I rinse out Betty's bowl and lean over to start filling it up. And what happens next happens so fast that I barely register it. In a blur of brown hair and white sundress, I see Jolene run past me and into the barn. She's shouting something back at Wells about how she's going to grab something for the puppy.

But she doesn't know Betty is technically loose, on

a lead that stretches to the middle of the damn barn. And Betty hasn't met Jolene. Betty is easily scared, and Jolene is a ball of hyper energy. I drop the bowl, water splashing all over my shoes as I take off inside. The hose is still running, but I don't care. I have to make sure Jolene isn't going to run right into Betty's path.

"Jolene!" Wells shouts, just as I see her running right toward Betty.

My feet move impossibly fast, and by the grace of god, I get to her before Betty does. I grab hold of Jolene's arm and swing her back, tugging her out of the way. I hold my other arm up to block us just as Betty growls and lunges. Jolene stumbles, making me lose my balance as my ankle twists. I fall down…hard.

And all I can think about is how all that work I've done for the past two weeks has gone up in smoke. Because she is not a bad dog. She is just terrified, and with someone unknown to her running straight at her while she eats…it was a recipe for disaster.

The wind is knocked out of me, and her teeth sink into my forearm with force but release quickly when she realizes who she's bitten. The pain is sharp and fucking brutal. My ankle is throbbing. Betty whines and backs up with her ears down.

I want to cry. My poor girl. No one will take her now. Not with a biting history, no matter how much it wasn't her fault.

God. Dammit.

CHAPTER TWENTY-FIVE

Poppy

"UNCLE WELLS!" Jolene shouts just as he rushes inside.

"Stop!" I tell him, holding on to my bloody forearm. "Let me put her back in. She doesn't need any more stimulus."

"You're bleeding!" Jolene yells, crying and hiccuping. Big fat tears are streaming down her face. The poor girl is a mess.

"I'm okay, Jolene. I promise, baby. I'm okay."

"Poppy, let me do it," Wells says, assertive and face all serious. "You're hurt. Wade, go get your grandmother. Now."

I'm already up on unsteady feet, hobbling toward Betty at a slow, measured pace. She's in the corner, and her ears are back. I'm in pain, but my heart is shattering for this poor girl, who was just taken by surprise. She was terrified, and that's no one's fault but those assholes we rescued her from.

"Hey, baby girl." My voice is quiet and calm. "I'm just gonna take that lead off of you, okay?"

My arm is dripping blood, and the sight of it is making me woozy. But I manage to get the lead unhooked and her bowl of food into her room. She looks at me with her big sad eyes, and I bite back tears.

"Hey, hey, whoa," Wells says, grabbing me as my feet stumble and I fall into the wall. My ankle is throbbing, and my vision has floaters in it. I am *not* good with blood.

"What happened?" Katherine all but shouts as she comes running into the barn.

"It's okay. I'm okay," I tell her. "Betty just got scared. It isn't anyone's fault. But I think I might need stitches."

Which is very unfortunate because my insurance here doesn't start until the two-month mark, and emergency room visits are not cheap.

"Let's get her in the car, Wells. Kids, can you be a big help and grab a bottle of water and open one of the car doors for us?"

"Maybe we could just go to the drugstore? I'm sure they sell those liquid stitches or whatever."

"No, you need a doctor." Wells' voice is strong and commanding, and I see far too much of his brother in him for my liking. Makes me wish Rhett were here.

"I don't have insurance yet." My cheeks flame.

"No worries about that," Katherine says. "We live in a small town, and that doctor owes us a favor."

Before I can say anything, Wells lifts me up into his arms. My stomach turns, the sudden shift in my body making me feel like I'm going to heave. I swallow past the dryness in my mouth and take a few deep breaths.

"I can walk," I manage to get out.

"Yeah, you look it," he says, rolling his eyes. "Just let me get you to the car. Momma will have to take you. I'll need to stay to take care of things. And…"

He trails off, side-eyeing me like he's afraid to say what's coming next.

"And…?"

"I'm gonna have to tell Rhett, Poppy."

"No." My voice is stronger than it has been for the past five minutes. "No way in hell."

"We have to tell him, dear." Katherine's soothing voice comes up behind us. "It's technically his ranch. He needs to know."

"And there ain't no way we're keeping those kids quiet. They're gonna run straight to him," Wells adds.

I want to cry. I want to curl up in a tight ball and just cry. This is *not* how today was supposed to go.

"Just…" I lower my voice, hoping only Wells can hear me. "Don't let him come to the hospital? Please?"

His worried gaze looks down at me with eyebrows drawn together before he sighs.

"Fine, Poppy. I'll try, okay? No guarantees. But I'll try."

Guess that's all I can hope for.

A whole afternoon and half an evening later, my arm is stitched up, and my ankle is wrapped. Thankfully, it's just a bad sprain, but he thinks I should stay off it for a week and let it fully heal. Little does he know, Momma didn't raise no pussy. I'll be back on it in no time, I'm sure.

The stitches have to be looked at in a week to make sure everything is healing correctly. I got IV antibiotics and some to take for the next week to make sure nothing gets infected. The best part, though? The pain meds he prescribed me. I cannot wait to get home and take some of those bad boys.

I insisted on paying at least for some of the visit, but the doctor was Katherine's friend, and he promised he was fine with treating this until my insurance kicked in.

The nurse wheels me out to the loading zone, where Katherine is waiting in her car. Except that's not her car, and that is definitely not Katherine standing next to it. Motherfucking fuck.

"No," I say, standing up out of the wheelchair.

"Poppy," he says in a warning tone.

"Can you call me a cab, please?" I use my best sugary voice. The nurse looks from me to Rhett and then back again.

"Thank you, Josie. We'll be fine from here."

"No we most certainly will not," I tell her, refusing to look back at Rhett. "Can you please call me a cab? Take pity on me, Josie. Would you want to get in that truck with that grumpy asshole?"

Her cheeks blush a bright red, and when she looks back at him, she looks like she's debating that answer a little too hard. Of course she would want to get in the truck with him. Look at him.

Christ's sake, Josie. Way to let me down.

"Come on, poppyseed." Suddenly, he's right beside me, lifting me into his arms like I can't walk.

"You and your brothers need to stop picking me up. I can walk just fine, thank you."

"Do you ever shut up?" he asks and then shuts the mother-loving door in my face.

"Excuse me?" I ask as he climbs in on his side. "God, get fucked, Rhett Black."

"I'd love to, Poppy. You offerin'?"

I go silent. If he's going to have a comeback for every little thing I say, maybe it'll shut him up if I shut up.

"Thank you for saving my baby girl today," he says quietly. "Wells told me what happened, that she was runnin' after something and didn't know that dog was out and about."

"She didn't," I whisper, my emotions and exhaustion getting the better of me. "It's not her fault. Or Wells'. It was just a freak accident."

"Bound to happen on a ranch. Can't count how many times my brothers and I got into trouble and wound up in this same hospital."

I nod my head but continue to stare out the window, resting my forehead on the glass. I'm so freaking tired down to my damn bones. I just want to somehow take a shower and then climb into bed and sleep for twelve hours. The truck goes quiet while we drive home, and I drift in and out of sleep. But when we pass the first driveway and then turn onto a road a bit farther down, I perk up.

"Where are we going?"

"My house." He states it like it should be the most obvious thing in the world.

"Why would we be going to your house?"

"Because you're hurt, and I don't like the idea of you alone in that house without any help. So you'll come stay with us until you can walk properly, and the kids and I will help out."

"You can't just kidnap me, Rhett. You can't just say we're going to talk and spend time together and then completely avoid me for a week and *still* expect me to just accept your help like this."

A noise comes out of his throat that sounds a lot like a growl mixed with a tired sigh. And I want to growl right back at him.

"Take me to my house. Wells or Hayes can come make sure I'm okay in the morning. I don't need your help."

"If you think I'm going to let one of my brothers be the one to care for you, you've got another thing coming, woman."

His house comes into sight, and I gape at it. I saw it from a distance on the tour, but up close, this place is gorgeous. And *huge*. What in the world does he need all this space for? I'm still staring at it open-mouthed when he gets out of the truck and comes around to my side.

"Please don't fight me, Poppy." His arms cage me into the truck, and I can't help but breathe in the fresh scent of him. And I notice for the first time that he looks tired…and worried?

"I'm not sleeping with you," I tell him.

"Momma set up the spare."

"Oh." Why am I sad about that? Did I really want him to insist I sleep with him? In his bed, in his room, in his house? Where his kids are? Because that's just stupid. How would we even explain that to them?

"So, you'll stay?"

I sigh. "Fine."

"Good." A wide smile breaks out across his face. "Because the kids have been a wreck since Momma carted you off to the hospital. They're gonna be waitin' at the front door for you."

That makes this very large pill a bit easier to swallow.

"Alright. And then I get a shower and a couple of those pain pills. Yeah?"

He tugs me out of the truck and into his arms. I let him. Partly because I'm too tired to walk and partly because I just want to be close to him.

"Only if you promise not to get all loopy and tear off my Wranglers again. Wouldn't want to take advantage of you in a weakened state."

I groan.

"Shut up."

CHAPTER TWENTY-SIX

Rhett

SHE'S RIGHT. I have been avoiding her. When I left that day, I wanted to meet with her later, or at least sometime this past week. I wanted to talk to her and kiss her and touch her all over again. But the second I got home and those two kids came runnin' up the front porch, reality hit me like a brick in the face.

She is twenty-six years old. A whole-ass decade younger than myself. And I'm supposed to just…what? Date her? Introduce her to my kids as my girlfriend? Shit. No twenty-six-year-old wants this kind of life.

"You're takin' that choice away from her," Hayes told me the other day in the barn. I hadn't spoken to either of them about what happened, but they obviously knew. I had taken his truck home, and I'd taken Poppy with me. It was easy to guess from there.

"Doesn't matter."

"It does. Because you're ruining your own damn happiness. And hers. You should let her choose."

I knew I couldn't avoid her forever. I had planned on giving the kids over to Momma one night this weekend and going over to talk to her. But then I saw Joey and Wade runnin' up over the hill, screaming and crying with Wells joggin' right behind. The look on his face said it all. Someone was hurt, and the only person he was working with all day was Poppy.

My stomach had dropped through my ass.

"She got bit," Joey had stuttered out between tears. "And it was all my fault!" She screamed and cried and carried on, with Wade joining her, even though I don't think he fully understood what was happening.

After I got them settled, I knew I needed to go get her. Wells had said it looked pretty bad and that she wasn't able to walk right because she had managed to twist her ankle on the way down. So I gave the kids over to Wells and headed to the hospital.

Momma tried to warn me that Poppy wouldn't be pleased to see me, but I wouldn't hear any of it. I was worried sick, pacing the floors at home until it was time to go get her. No matter how stubborn she was, I knew she'd give in.

And now, with her in my house and in my bathtub, I know I made the right decision. I know she's safe. I know if anything happens, I'm here. Literally, I'm right here. I'm sitting on the bedroom floor with my back against the bathroom door, listening to her soak her pains away.

She took some pain meds right before I drew her the bath, so I know she's got to be feeling the effects by now. She's in there humming to herself, and every once in a while, I hear her sigh. Damn, it feels nice to have her in my home. It feels right.

I knock softly on the door.

"Y'alright in there? Ready to get out?"

She groans. "I guess."

We both came to the realization quickly that she was not able to undress or dress herself without the threat of fallin' over. It took some convincing, but eventually, she let me help her out of her dirty clothes and into the bath. And I know she's stuck in that thing now until I get in there to help her out.

Swallowing hard, because my cock is already solid as stone, I stand up and slip inside. I don't want to let any of the heat out, but goddamn, she's steamed it up in here. Her hair has faded a bit since the first time I saw her, and while she looks beautiful no matter what, I do find myself missing that bright peachy color.

"No peeking." She crosses her arms over her breasts, but all it does is push them together. My dick twitches.

"Too late."

She groans. I bite back laughter, trying not to push all of her buttons, but the girl makes it too damn easy.

So I grab a towel off the counter and lay it over the tub. Grabbing her gently under her arms, I help her stand up on her good foot. The water sloshes out onto the floor, and she looks like it pains her to make a mess. But I don't care. All I care about is getting her wrapped up and warm.

"Alright, careful steppin' out."

It takes a good chunk of time, but eventually, she's in an oversized T-shirt, some shorts that are way too tight on that perfect ass, and no bra. I want to see her like this every night. I want to be lying in bed waiting for her to walk out of that bathroom and ride my cock every goddamn night.

"Alright, I need to wrap my ankle up again," she says, limping toward my bedroom door. But I don't let her get there. I swoop her up and plant her ass on my bed. Sure, I had the guest room made up for her, but I'm not that strong. I thought I was, but I'm not. She's going to be in my house, she's going to be sleepin' with me. I'll figure out the kids later.

"What're you doing?" She tries to slide off the bed, but I block her way.

"I'm puttin' you to bed, poppyseed. Now, lie back and let me wrap that ankle so you can get some sleep."

"I am *not* sleeping in your bed."

I grunt, knowing it's secretly her favorite part about me, and just stand there. I know I'll win this little fight because she can't get up and run away this time. Is that unfair? Maybe, but I can't bring myself to care. I tell myself I just need her in here in case she needs something in the middle of the night. I can keep a better eye on her here.

"Rhett." She sighs. "I'm too high on pain pills to fight with you. So I am going to let you wrap my ankle, and I'm going to let you make me sleep in this bed. But no funny business." She points a mean finger in my direction.

I just roll my eyes and wait for her to lean back before going to hunt down the extra wraps the doctor sent her home with. She kept her hurt arm out of the water for tonight, so we can check the stitches and clean them in the morning. I'm about to tell her as much when I get back to my room, but she's fast asleep.

I don't want to let her go the night without having her ankle wrapped, so I carefully sit at the foot of the bed and slowly wrap the stretchy brown fabric around her bruised ankle and down to her swollen foot. Her toes are still painted a bright pink, and it's a strange contrast to the yellow and purple bloomin' on her skin.

"You're being nice to me," she whispers, still half-asleep. Her eyes are shut.

"Mhm," I hum. "Don't get used to it."

A little smile graces her pretty lips, and then they part on the loudest fucking snore I have ever heard in my dang life. I don't even think Hayes snores that loud when he's drunk. Shit, she may wake my damn kids.

Biting back laughter and hoping I have earplugs somewhere in this house, I pin off the wrap and carefully tuck her under the covers. She rolls to the side and throws an arm across my pillow. It reminds me of how she slept half on my body after the other night. I got to fall asleep and wake up to the sweet scent of her shampoo.

I lean over and kiss her forehead.

"Good night, Poppy."

CHAPTER TWENTY-SEVEN

Poppy

RHETT'S *beard scratches against my skin as he slides down my body, kissing all the parts of me that I'm most self-conscious about. He spreads my legs, carefully making sure that my ankle remains in a comfortable position, and then slowly licks me through my slit.*

I moan and relax into the bed as he works me over, leisurely licking and sucking. It's like he's just down there to enjoy himself, not rushing to get me to finish. He's building the pleasure, pulling away when I get too close and driving me mad each time he does it.

And then the tip of his finger teases my entrance before slowly slipping inside. My hips rise off the bed and try to get more. I'm greedy. I want it all.

"Rhett." God, I love moaning his name. It urges him on, making him give me what I want.

"That's it, baby. I love hearing you moan my name."

I jolt awake and find him grinning up at me from between my thighs. And then he makes an obscene show of licking through my folds before taking my clit into his mouth and sucking hard.

"What're you doing?" I whisper-yell, knowing the kids could walk in at any moment. I glance toward the door and then back at him, fighting the growing urge to come. Christ, he's good with his mouth.

"What does it feel like I'm doing? The door is locked, don't worry," he murmurs against my skin. "Lie back and let me make you feel good."

I do as he says because worrying about what we are or if his kids are going to start pounding on that door is too much for this early in the morning. One more orgasm, and then no more of this until we talk.

My hands curl through his hair, tugging on the soft strands as he works my body over like an instrument he's been playing for years. His strong arms wrap around my middle, holding me to him, and within minutes, I'm biting down on my fist to keep myself from crying out my orgasm.

Rhett crawls back up my body and lets his hips rest on mine while he cages me in with his arms. He wipes his beard, smirking before leaning down to kiss me. I can taste myself on his lips, and it surprises me that I don't mind it. If anything, it makes me want to take this further and give his very hard cock some relief. I lift my hips and grind against him.

"You're hurt," he says, kissing my cheek and then down my neck. "Plus, I am so desperate for you, Poppy, that if I fuck you, I will pound this bed through the goddamn wall."

Holy shit.

"Your moods give me whiplash, Rhett Black."

He ignores me and rolls off the bed, his cock straining against the tight black briefs he's wearing. God, his body is cut from stone. You cannot convince me otherwise.

"Let's get your stitches cleaned and your bandage changed. Then we can make some breakfast with the kids."

"Do you not have to work?" I watch him get dressed, fascinated by how sexy it is just to watch his back flex as he puts on a T-shirt.

"Nah, told Momma I was taking care of you for the week. The guys will have it under control."

"So…" I look around his room, suddenly realizing I'm in my own clothes, but I have no idea where he got them from. I don't see a suitcase or bag lying around anywhere. "Where are my things? You must've had someone bring my stuff over. I need a bra. I don't really think I should be walking around tits out."

"But I like it when your tits are out." A sly grin forms on his lips, and I can't help but roll my eyes.

"Rhett," I groan.

"Momma packed you a bag. It's in the spare." He tugs on some jeans. "I'll go grab it."

He walks out without another word. Like I said…whiplash.

"Poppy!" Jolene and Wade both shout my name and come running over to where Rhett perched me on the couch. My stitches have been cleaned, and a bra has been secured.

"Careful of her arm and ankle!" Rhett calls from the kitchen. They both slow down and carefully climb onto the couch. Jolene plops herself right on my lap. Her little hands grab hold of my cheeks.

"I'm sorry I got you hurt." She looks like she's about to cry all over again, so I wrap her up in my arms and pull her in for a hug.

"You didn't get me hurt, sweetheart." I stroke her bed head. "Your Uncle Wells and I didn't communicate with either of you that Betty might be out. And Betty didn't know you and got scared."

"Accidents happen," Wade says with all of his five-year-old knowledge.

"Yes, they do." I smile at him and reach out to hold his hand. Jolene stays tucked into my chest, her fingers playing with the ends of my hair that desperately needs to be freshened up.

Which reminds me…

"Wells was going to take me into town sometime this weekend. I need to get some stuff," I call out to Rhett. "Can you get my phone so I can text him?"

"No."

I sigh. I do not want to fight with him in front of his kids, but I will.

"Rhett."

"I'll take you today." Color me surprised. He's actually going to do me a favor.

"Can we come?" Both of the kids shout in unison, Jolene's head popping up from my chest to look at her daddy in the kitchen.

He turns around from where he's frying bacon and points his tongs at both of them.

"Only if we can get ice cream."

"Of course we can get ice cream!" Wade shouts.

Jolene squeals and shakes my shoulders.

"Ice cream!" she sings.

Rhett laughs at both of them, and it looks like his heart is going to explode from how much he loves them. There's a lot of things you can say about Rhett, and not a lot of those are good things. But you can't fault him for how much he loves his kids. Just seeing them interact for the last two weeks has made me realize that for how grumpy he may be on the outside, this man has a soft, gooey center reserved especially for his kids.

Am I attracted to a hot single dad? Is that what this is? He makes me want to slap him on a daily basis, but when I see him interact with his kids, my heart wants to explode. It's the most attractive thing I think I've ever seen.

And when he goes from looking at them to winking at me, I think I'm doomed.

Because I think I want this. The kids on my lap, the man in the kitchen, and the promise of ice cream. Sounds like a pretty good life to me. It sounds settled and happy and everything I haven't had.

CHAPTER TWENTY-EIGHT

Rhett

AFTER SPENDING the morning shopping for everything under the damn sun, she's now in the downstairs bathroom, letting her hair sit in pink dye while she does the same to Joey's. And don't think for a second that Wade is left out because they all convinced me to let Wade get some purple.

"It won't show up as bright as mine," she told them both, trying to manage their hopes. "I have blonde hair, and you guys have gorgeous brown hair. That means it'll be darker on you."

They're still so excited, sitting on the bathroom counter while Poppy sits behind on a barstool and paints their hair wild colors. I didn't even want to let her dye her own hair, let alone the kids, with how bad her arm is swollen. I know that shit hurts, but that woman is more stubborn than a dang mule sometimes.

I'm leaning against the doorframe, listening to them chatter about their friends at school, how they were excited to be out for the summer, and how they spend their days with Momma. Poppy takes it all in, looking at each of them as they speak in the mirror. My heart swells with pride at these two kids. They're brilliant, funny, and so fucking cute it makes my chest hurt.

Their momma has no fucking clue what she lost when she left them. But Poppy…she laughs at their jokes and talks to them like she's genuinely interested in their lives. And I don't think it's a front. I think she actually *likes* my kids. And I know they like her. Anytime she isn't around, all they can talk about is Poppy this and Poppy that. They beg me to go play with her and talk about all the things they get to do when they take her lunch.

I'd be lying if I said I don't do the same. Every day since the first day I saw her, all I can think about is her. Sometimes I'm angry, sometimes I'm turned on, but more often than not, I just *miss her*. And I fight that feeling every damn day. I can't get too close to her. I won't let her break my kids' hearts.

But then she walks around my house in tight shorts and bends over when she knows I'm looking. And then she laughs at something Wade says so hard she snorts before resting her hand on my arm like it's the most natural thing in the world. She walks around outside barefoot with her crutch, bending over to pick up wildflowers when she finds them to braid into Joey's hair.

And I'm gone all over again. I can't escape her. I can't escape this feeling.

"Daddy! Hello!"

Joey is waving at me like I've been staring off into space. But I haven't been. I've been staring at Poppy. She smirks as she makes sure the towel around Joey's neck is clipped shut.

"Yes, baby girl?"

"Mine is done. We just have to let it sit. What do you think?" She hops off the counter, and Wade scoots into her previous spot. I look down at her with her forehead stained pink and her dark brown hair looking more maroon than pink.

"I think you're gonna look gorgeous."

She smiles, all happiness and excitement for tryin' something new.

"I know." She shrugs and then takes off into the kitchen, yellin' about being hungry.

"You better go fetch her," Poppy tells me, a genuine smile on her face that makes her pretty eyes shine. "That pink dye gets on your pretty hardwood floors or white countertops, I'm not sure how easily it's gonna come up."

I shrug. "If the biggest thing I have to worry about in life is some pink hair dye droppin' on the floor or a pink handprint on my countertop, I think I'm doin' alright, poppyseed."

"That would've been nice to hear growing up." Her face turns a bit sad. She's still masking it with a smile, but I can see it in her eyes that she's thinking back on something that isn't pleasant.

"Angry parents?" I ask.

She hums and nods. "Dad wasn't around much and left by the time I was ten. Mom worked hard to take care of me, but I come from a small town riddled with…" She trails off, looking at Wade and then back to me. "Riddled with people who *eat too much candy* and hardly any jobs available."

"Ah." I nod sympathetically. I'm not sure what else to say. I want to ask her more about her mom, like if she was someone who *ate too much candy* or if she was able to stay clean for Poppy. But I don't. This isn't a conversation you have when your five-year-old is present.

"Anyway." She sighs. "I swear my mom loved a clean house more than she loved me. If I spilled water, I was in trouble. If I left a cup out, I was in trouble. It was a make-your-bed-every-morning type of household."

"I never make my bed," Wade says as he plays with his toes. "And I spilled milk once, but Daddy didn't care. He just helped me clean it up."

"That's because you have the best daddy there is." She smiles at him in the mirror, and then like it's the most natural thing in the world, she leans forward and kisses him on the cheek.

Neither one of them notices what she's done, and maybe it's not actually a big deal. But to me? The breath is knocked out of me. I don't even think their momma ever loved on them like that. Especially not Wade. She never wanted a boy, and when he came out screaming, I could see the annoyance on her face.

But now he's giggling as she blows raspberries on his cheek and neck. His face turns red as he tries to bat her away, and her face gets absolutely covered in purple hair dye.

"Say uncle! Say uncle!" he shouts, tickling her neck with his chubby fingers.

"Okay, okay!" she cries out playfully. "Uncle!"

She picks up an old rag and wipes violently at the dye on her face, but I think it's going to be stuck there until she showers.

"You seem to have patience with my two monsters," I say once they've both settled down and she's back to work on his hair. "Growin' up like that make you wanna be the opposite?"

"God, yes." She groans. "I always told myself I was not going to be like her. When I had kids, they would know that they were loved more than the material things we filled our house with. They were going to be put first. Their joy and laughter should fill a home, not things."

I was gonna have to walk out of this bathroom before I got down on one knee for this woman. Jesus wept, she has me tangled up in knots. The way she talks about family and happiness…that's the kind of life I want. That's the kind of life I strive to give to my kids. And the fact that she wants exactly that makes me want her all the more.

"You want kids?" I can't help myself.

"Yes." Her eyes light up again when she looks over at me. "A whole horde of them. I've always known I want kids. It's why I was a nanny for the past couple years. Figured it would actually be a job I enjoyed. Just didn't anticipate how hard it would be to leave them when the job was done."

Her voice cracks, and I can see the unshed tears glistening in her eyes. I can't even imagine what it would be like to grow that close to kids and then have to leave them for another job. I know these two are my own, but if I had to leave them for any reason, it would feel like someone took my heart out of my chest and stomped on it with their boot.

And I can't help myself. I know my kid is sittin' on the counter in front of us, and I know I shouldn't show any type of affection in front of them when we haven't even begun whatever the hell is happenin' between us. But she's sad, and it's breaking my heart in two.

So I take a couple of steps over to her, closing the distance between us, and I rub her back in soothing circles and then bring her clean hand to my mouth for a kiss. I'd kiss her hair, but unlike my children, I don't want to be covered in hair dye. The guys would never let me live it down.

She leans into my touch and gives me one of her sweet Poppy smiles before I hear something crash in the kitchen.

"Wanna bet your sister tried to reach something she shouldn't again?" I ask Wade.

He just snickers and nods.

"Yeah, me too, buddy. I'll be back." Turning to Poppy, I ask, "You okay?"

"Yeah, fine. I'm almost done here, and then I'll wash my hair before we wash theirs."

"Shower party!" Wade shouts, his arms flying up in the air.

If only I could have a shower party with Poppy... alone. In a house where for one night, we don't have to worry about kids popping in at any given moment. That's the kind of shower party *I* want.

CHAPTER TWENTY-NINE

Rhett

WE FALL into bed together after the kids have been put down for the night. Their freshly colored hair was the only thing they wanted to talk about: when they could try a different color, when they would be old enough to bleach their hair like Poppy's, or when they could go to their grandparents' house to show it all off.

But now Poppy is in my bed again, and she's all I can think about. I helped her shower and completely failed *not* getting a boner in the process. As she scoots closer, wrapping herself around my body, the scent of her shampoo fills my space.

"I think we should take care of this," she whispers, running one of her hands down my stomach and under my shorts. Her soft hand wraps around me, and my hips press forward, desperate for the attention.

"You gonna let me back inside that sweet cunt,

Poppy?" I grab the side of her face and kiss her hard, pouring all of my feelings and emotions into that kiss that I'm too scared to tell her. Everything I've been feeling over the past week spills into the way we're kissing.

We move quickly, our sleep clothes getting thrown to the floor and her leg getting tossed over my hip. My cock lines up with her slit, and I tease her for just a moment before sinking inside of her. She takes me to the hilt in one go, moaning in my ear as she stretches around me. Such a tight fuckin' fit.

"You were made for my cock. Do you know that, poppyseed?" I kiss her. "Made just for me."

"Just for you." She pants.

What I thought would be hot and fast turns into something completely different. I slowly move in and out of her, letting her feel every bit of me each time. We kiss and cling to each other, our breaths mixing as our mouths move together.

"You're so beautiful." I push her pretty pink hair out of her face and make her look at me. "You're goddamn gorgeous. Everything about you. From the way you smile to the way you treat my kids. Fuck, Poppy. You're so fucking special."

The words flow out of me before I can catch them. I've never been like this with anyone, not even my ex. Something about this woman makes my heart beat so hard I think it's going to fly out of my chest. And when she grabs my face and her eyes are watery, I know she feels the same. There's something happening here, something big and scary and too much.

"I like you, too, Rhett Black," she says, pulling me impossibly closer. "Especially when you're not being an ass."

I laugh and kiss her hard, sweeping my tongue across hers to keep me from blurting out all of the things racing through my heart and mind.

Fuck me. I'm gonna fall in love with this woman.

Grabbing her ass, I hold her flush to my body as I pick up speed. I can feel her getting close, and I'm struggling to hold out. It just seems to be like this with her, where she gets me so worked up I lose all sense of self-control.

"Yes." She whimpers, and her teeth bite down on my shoulder. "Yes, Rhett. Fuck."

Hearing my name on her lips is enough to push me over the edge, and thank god she's there, too. I don't think I could've held out. I spill inside of her, an image of her pregnant flashing through my mind briefly before I stuff that down…way, way the fuck down.

Jesus Christ, what is wrong with me?

We lie here, breathing heavily and holding each other until I can feel myself leaking out of her. So I clean her up and then help her get dressed before slipping on my own clothes. The thing about having kids is knowing you should be dressed at all times. You never know when you're gonna have someone with a nightmare or, heaven forbid, the damn house catches fire.

That's a recurring nightmare I have.

"I'm sorry about the sappy story earlier," she says, breaking the silence. "I can get a little emotional when I have to talk about my mom."

She rolls over and lays her head on my chest, and I wrap my arm around her to give her any kind of comfort I can.

"It's okay. I screamed at you over my sister's apron. So..." I huff or grunt or somethin', I don't know. I'm not great at admitting when I'm wrong.

She laughs softly. "It's okay, Rhett. I can't imagine what was going through your head when you saw me standing there. I felt awful."

"I've done all of this for Addie. Every rescue animal I bring onto this damn ranch is for her. She always wanted it, and this is the only way I can keep her close." I sigh and kiss the top of her head. "I'm so sorry for yellin' at you."

"It was Addie's dream to run a rescue?" She moves her head so that she can look at my face.

I nod. "Always loved animals. She was bringing something home every damn day. Pretty sure she adopted everything from a duck to a dog."

"That's so cute. She had a big heart."

"She did." I clear my throat of the tears threatenin' to fall again. I haven't let myself feel this much about

Addie since she passed. I've had too much goin' on between the shit with my ex and Dean being in and out of rehab. Not to mention running the whole damn ranch. My shoulders are fucking heavy with it all.

I'm ready to change the damn subject.

"You got any siblings?"

"Nope." She pops the *p*. "I think that's another reason I've always wanted kids. It was lonely growing up without anyone to play with. I mean, sure, I had friends. But Mom was always gone working, and I had the house to myself every day after my dad left. So it was quiet."

"Never quiet here," I grunt.

"No, it's not." I can feel her smile against her chest. "You're a great dad, Rhett. Those kids love you to the moon and back."

"They're pretty fond of you as well, you know."

"Yeah?" She looks up at me again, hope shining in her hazel eyes. "I like them, too. Good kids. Funny as hell."

"Wells tell you about the adoption event in a few weeks?"

"Yes, I'm so excited! It's on my birthday weekend."

"You tell him that? Because he's gonna tell the whole damn ranch."

She laughs. "Yeah, he said something about getting drunk and making a bonfire? Is that what you country folks do for fun around here?"

"Something like that. Momma will bake you a big ole cake, and everyone that works here will hang around for the party. We can do it after the event."

"You will all be exhausted. That's silly to spend all that energy on me."

"Try tellin' Momma that."

She huffs out a quiet laugh, and then the conversation just kind of dissolves. I rack my brain for anything to talk about because I don't want this little bubble we have right now to go away. I'm desperate to keep her talking about anything, but those pain meds hit her hard, and she's passed out on top of me.

I've gotta say, it's not the most comfortable position we could be lyin' in. And I'd love nothing more than to adjust and get more comfortable. But I don't want to wake her up. Her breath fans across my chest, and her arm is thrown across my stomach, with her hand tucked under my back.

I'm not sure how we got here, sleeping together in my bed. We didn't even *try* her sleeping in the spare. The kids didn't ask any questions today when they saw the spare bedroom still pristine. Granted, they're kids, so they probably didn't even notice. But the longer this goes and the more I fall for this girl wrapped in my arms, the more likely it is they'll see something they aren't used to seeing.

Kids may be oblivious to a lot of things, but they're also incredibly perceptive of the bigger things. And whatever is happening between me and Poppy is bigger than anything they've experienced since the split. They're bound to see a change in me soon, and I'm gonna have to figure out what exactly I'm going to say.

And what Poppy *wants* me to say.

CHAPTER THIRTY

Poppy

IT'S BEEN an entire week of sitting on my ass, watching movies with the kids while Rhett supervises and hovers. He's barely let me walk around the yard, let alone go back to work. But we had my checkup today, and the doctor has given me the green light to finally go back. Rhett stood there and grunted the entire time, but he's not going to keep me captive anymore.

I'm ready to get back to Betty.

I've been begging Wells for updates on her every day, and every day, he tells me the same thing. She's scared, cowering in the corner when he comes over to feed her or sit with her. She's not even gone outside to potty anymore. My poor girl needs me to come back and break her back out of her shell. And I need to let her know that I'm okay.

Don't get me wrong, living with Rhett for the past

week has been…oddly fun. I mean, I knew the sex would be fun. We clicked on that *right away*. But if anyone had asked me a few weeks ago if I would be living with the man, I would've laughed in their faces. The last thing I would have wanted to do was live with him. Fuck him, maybe. The attraction was fast and strong. But I couldn't stand the guy.

Barely can now. But still, there's something different about him — now that I've gotten to know him.

"Not much of a limp anymore," Wells says, all smiles when I walk through the front door of Katherine and Clyde's. It's Saturday dinner, and I'm stoked to be out of the house. The kids run past me with their overnight bags hanging from their shoulders. They drop them in the hallway and run off to find their grandparents.

"Hey! Can we maybe not just leave our bags in the hallway?" I shout after them, smiling when they run back and pick them up, saying sorry as they put them on the bench instead. Wells gives me a look, and I know what he's thinking. Since when did I become…this?

"Doctor says I can come back this week," I tell him, ignoring the look.

"That means you can come dancing!" Hayes sings out, poking his head around the corner.

"No, that means she's still resting for two more nights before she goes back to work." Rhett's gruff voice sends a shiver down my spine, and I know what he's thinking. If they're going out and the kids are with his parents, that leaves us alone in the house.

Finally.

"You're such a party pooper," Hayes says, following us into the kitchen.

"You've been hiding her all week," Wells adds.

"Poppy!" Katherine walks over and wraps me in her arms, her familiar flour-and-vanilla scent wrapping me up. "You look so much better. How's that bite?"

"Much better, thank you."

I walk over to the table, and Rhett is right there, pulling out a chair for me to sit down.

"Quit hovering." I slap him on the arm. "I'm fine. I can barely even feel it anymore."

He grunts. Shocker.

"Just because you're not goin' out tonight doesn't mean we can't stay here...right?" Wade's little voice floats in from the living room.

"You are always welcome here!" Clyde tells him. "You know that. It'll give your daddy a break."

He winks at both of us, and I'm ready for the world to swallow me whole.

"Bro..." Hayes is eyeing Wade from where he leans against the countertop. "Is your hair purple?"

Wade just giggles.

"Mine is pink!" Jolene jumps into view. "We wanted to see how long it would take you to notice!"

"That is the coolest!" Wells walks over to him and

kneels down in front of him. "Think I'd look good with purple hair?" He looks over to Jolene. "Or pink? Hell, I kind of want pink."

"Poppy can do it! She's great at it!" Jolene is bouncing on her tiptoes.

"Why didn't she do your daddy's, then?" Hayes asks, grinning like an idiot. Rhett turns to give him a look of death.

"Daddy's hair is too dark. It wouldn't have shown up," Wade answers.

Hayes and Wade both continue to give Rhett shit for the rest of the night, but he takes it on the chin. I guess he's grown up with his brothers picking on him his entire life, so he has a bit more patience with them than he has with me. The last time I got smart with him, he spanked me until my ass was red.

That was a fun night.

"Come on," Wells begs. "Come out with us. Take your woman out."

"Not my woman." He says it a bit too quickly, and I know he can see the change in my demeanor. I don't know what I expected him to say, because we *still* haven't talked about what we are. But I didn't expect him to dismiss me so quickly.

"Okay," Hayes drawls. "We'll leave you to whatever it is you're going to be doing with *not* your woman."

We watch them drive away, and when they're out of sight, Rhett puts his arm around my shoulders and leads me off toward his house. I want to slink him off because I want to pout. The little girl inside of me that is far too accustomed to being left is hurt. But the grown woman I've worked hard to become is trying not to let it get to her.

I'm an adult, and I can handle whatever this is.

"We have the house to ourselves," he says, his voice deep and raspy. His breath is warm on my hair as he kisses my temple.

"And what should we do with all this newfound freedom?"

"I can think of a few things..." He leans down and kisses my neck until it tickles, and I pull away.

"Okay, whatever you have on your mind, I am totally down for. But at the rate I'm walking, it's going to take us all night to get home." Because while I'm not in as much pain, I still struggle to walk normally. So I tug him to a stop and then stand behind him, gesturing for him to bend down.

"A piggyback ride?" he asks, his eyebrow raised.

"Sure." I shrug, grinning at him. "Now, bend over, cowboy. I need a ride."

CHAPTER THIRTY-ONE

Poppy

HE SETS me down on the front porch, making sure I don't put too much weight on my ankle. Such a worry-wart. I've told him multiple times a day over the past few that I'm really not hurting anymore. He holds open the door, and I hike up my jeans from where they fell as we walked over.

"You paint them britches on?"

I snort.

"Britches? How old are you, Rhett Black?" He gives me a look. "I'm just sayin'. I'm all for dating an older man, but even I have my limits."

"Poppy," he says with a warning tone. "Keep that shit up and I'll put you over my knees again."

"Oh, no," I say sarcastically, slinking past him into the house. "We wouldn't want that, would we?"

"I knew you liked it." He walks slowly toward me

until my back is up against the wall. "You like it when I spank this ass, Poppy?"

He grabs a handful of ass, his fingers digging into my flesh through the denim. I can't bite back the moan as I push my hips forward and wrap my hands around the back of his neck. I tug him down and kiss him, biting his lower lip when he pulls away.

"I like anything you do to me, cowboy."

He grabs my wrists and wraps one of his hands around them, holding them above my head against the wall. My breasts push forward, and he gets distracted for a moment. I purposefully wore something a little more low-cut tonight. Lately, I've been stuck in oversized T-shirts and shorts with my hair pulled up and no makeup on. There's not really been a point to getting ready when Rhett won't let me do anything other than rest.

So tonight, I wanted to make a bit of an effort. I curled my hair and put a little makeup on. The *britches* I'm wearing are my favorite pair and make my ass look like a damn peach. I even wore my new cowgirl boots I ordered online. Rhett had made fun of me for it when they arrived the other day, but I think he secretly likes them. He wouldn't stop staring at me when I put them on.

"Do you like it when I'm in control, poppyseed?" His hand squeezes my wrists.

All I can do is nod. His voice has taken on a new

quality that is doing all sorts of things to me. It's deep and commanding, and I'm wondering where this is going.

"Good girl." He leans down and lifts me into his arms. I love how easily he can lift me up and throw me around. From the second he threw me over his shoulder that day and plopped me up on his horse like I weighed no more than a feather, there was a part of me that knew I was a fucking goner.

He kisses me the entire way up to his bedroom before tossing me on his bed. I bounce a couple of times, and then he's on me, undressing me like it's his only mission in life. Within seconds, I'm naked on the bed, and he's tugging his shirt over his head in my favorite way. God, it's sexy when he does it in one fell swoop.

I scoot toward the headboard, getting comfortable as he watches me. When I spread my thighs, he stands there frozen, licking his lips while I begin to play with myself. I'm already wet, my body ready for our night of fun together.

Rhett walks over to his closet and disappears for a second. I stop playing and rise up on my elbows, trying to get a look at what he's doing. And when he finally walks back out, there's a long black rope in his hands. My pussy clenches with excitement.

"Oh, how cliché," I tease. "A cowboy who likes to play with rope."

"Poppy," he says, a wicked smile playing across his lips. "Shut up and put your hands on the headboard."

I do as I'm told, and he ties my hands together before attaching the rope to the headboard. A thrill runs through me from being at his mercy like this. Testing the rope, I realize he's tied it tight enough that I can't move, but if I wanted to slip free, I probably could. That makes me feel a bit better.

"This okay, Poppy?" he asks as he unbuttons his jeans. The white band of his boxers peeks out, and I lick my lips. God, his body is perfect. I love everything about it. From the dark hair on his chest and stomach to the sharp angles of his hips that point downward to his giant cock. Fuck, he's a work of damn art.

I nod.

"Words."

I roll my eyes. "Yes, it's fine."

He tsks me. "That's gonna cost you. Any bit of attitude I see tonight earns that ass a hard whack."

"Promises, promises." I roll over and wiggle my ass into the air, testing and teasing him.

He wastes no time, and his hand lands hard on my ass cheek, making me yelp into the pillow. When he swings again, landing on the other cheek, that pain turns to pleasure. Never fancied myself as this type of girl, but I love the little bites of pain he gives me, especially when he's all moody and in control like he is now.

"I'm going to make good on the promise I made

earlier this week," he says, kicking the rest of his clothes off. I watch him as he climbs onto the bed, and then he's behind me, kneeling between my legs and spreading my cheeks.

"Which is?" I ask, a bit breathless. I love it when he's so blatant while *looking* at me. His thumbs press into my lips and tease my entrance. He blows cool air across my slit, and I can't help but push back toward him. I'm desperate for his touch.

"I'm going to fuck you so hard and so deep that this bed cracks the damn drywall."

I groan. Fuck, the mouth on this man. It makes me impossibly wet, and he notices. His fingers tease me, sliding between my folds and collecting my slickness before circling my clit. It pulls a whimper from my lips, and he chuckles as those two fingers sink inside of me.

"You are a needy little thing, aren't you, poppyseed?"

"Fuck." I moan when he curls those thick digits inside of me. He finds my spot with ease, curling against it and throwing me violently toward the edge.

"That's it." He smacks my ass with his free hand and then massages the sore flesh. "Be loud for me, Poppy. We have the house to ourselves, and I intend on making you scream until you're hoarse."

"Jesus Christ!" I shout out when he adds another finger while his thumb circles my clit. I'm stretched and full and so fucking close. I scream his name along with some expletives as he continues his assault on my pussy.

"Say my name," he demands as he smacks me again. "Say my fucking name, Poppy."

"Rhett!" I shout, my pussy spasming against his fingers. They keep going, pulling every ounce of pleasure from my body. My legs are shaking, and I'm struggling to keep myself up.

"Again," he commands, spanking me *hard* this time. That sharp sting goes right to my clit, and it's painful, but fuck if I'm not coming *again*.

"Rhett! Fuck!"

"That's right, baby. So fucking sexy. I love hearing my name on those pretty lips."

He slows his thrusting, and the mattress dips as he readjusts himself. I'm too out of it to realize what he's doing before his hands grab my hips, and he yanks my pussy down onto his face. He's lying on his back beneath me, and he gives me long, slow licks.

"Oh, god." I moan and grind against his mouth. His tongue dips inside of me and then sucks hard on my sensitive nub. "Oh, god!" I shout. "I can't come again, Rhett. I can't."

I try to pull away, but he holds me to his face.

"Then don't," he murmurs. "This is for me, poppy-seed. I needed to taste you. Just let me."

I do. I relax into the bed and let the rope hold me in position. My hips move slowly against him as he licks and sucks. His teeth graze my clit, and then he's sucking and biting on my pussy lips. He eats me like I'm his last meal, like he's starved for me. I worry about his breathing, but it feels too fucking good to move or fight his grip.

I figure if he needs to breathe, he'll tap out.

Rhett's hands grab my ass and thighs. God, I love the way his hands massage my body, like he could lie here all fucking day just touching and licking me. I thought I was too sensitive for another orgasm, but after what feels like hours of his licking, the heat starts to build again. My body has relaxed against him, and it wants more.

"This pussy tastes so fucking good, Poppy," he says, slipping out from under me. I can't help but make a pathetic noise. "I could have stayed there all goddamn night, licking you to orgasm after orgasm. But I made a promise."

"To fuck me into the drywall?" I ask, partially teasing and partially hoping he's about to make good on it.

He hums. "And what kind of man would I be if I didn't keep my promises?"

"A shitty one."

He laughs.

"Exactly."

CHAPTER THIRTY-TWO

Poppy

HE MAKES good on his promise. He thrusts deep, not giving me much time to adjust before he's slipping out and plowing back in. Rhett fills me like no other man ever has, and the stretch of it sends me into fucking euphoria.

He hisses through his teeth, bottoming out and holding himself there for a moment. My pussy twitches around his girth, already ready for another orgasm. His hand reaches around to play with my clit, and I squeeze the absolute life out of him. I'm so sensitive.

"Poppy," he grunts. "This cunt is perfection."

His rhythm picks back up, and the headboard begins to smack against the wall. The mattress groans beneath us with each forward thrust, and I'm a little concerned we might break his damn bed. His skin is slapping against my own, and the sound my wetness makes is enough to make a girl blush.

"You ready for me, Poppy?" His fingers dig into the flesh of my hips as his cock touches the very end of me. He's so goddamn *deep*. And from this angle, I can feel every sweet inch of him.

"Yes." My fingers wrap around the rope as I attempt to hold myself up. He's literally fucking me into the mattress.

"You gonna come for me, beautiful woman?" A hard smack hits my ass, and the banging of the bed against the wall becomes obnoxious.

"Yes," I moan. "You're so deep, Rhett. Oh, my god."

"That's right, poppyseed. I own this pussy." He smacks my ass again and then pinches my clit between his fingers. "Come for me."

I'm gone. I scream, and if anyone else were to hear it, they'd probably think it was a dying animal. I don't hold back, letting all of the pleasure and pain and emotions flood out of me. Rhett keeps going until his hips stutter and then stop. I can feel him empty into me, his cum filling me up. Never did I think that I, Poppy Sharpe, would have a breeding kink, but god damn, the thought of him getting me pregnant makes me hot.

I collapse into the mattress, my body no longer able to hold me up. My limbs shake, and my wrists burn from the rope. Rhett wastes no time once he's finished untying my hands from the headboard. I roll over, and his big hands work the blood back into my fingers as his cum begins to leak out of me.

"Washcloth!" I beg as I clench. "Leaking here."

"Oh?"

He slinks down my body and pries my legs apart. I can feel it slide between my cheeks. A moment later, his fingers are there, swiping from my ass to my pussy and then slipping inside.

"That's where it belongs," he murmurs, making me feel a bit light-headed. Between the pressure building between my thighs and his possessive thoughts, I'm struggling to breathe.

"You're a little possessive."

He chuckles, dark and deep.

"Because it's all mine."

I try not to think too far into that and fail miserably. I've never had someone claim me like this. My mind wants to make excuses, like he only does it when we're in bed together. But that's not true. He openly staked his claim in the bar, and he hasn't been shy about touching me in front of his family.

But we *still* haven't talked. And I know that's partially my fault. I need to push the issue, make him talk to me so we can sort this out. I'm just afraid of what the answer's going to be. Partly because I don't want to be embarrassed...I don't want to be the young girl chasing after the older guy. But mainly I'm scared that I will feel more than him, and that'll break a little piece of my heart.

"Shower?" he asks, looking up from between my legs.

I smile and sigh. "Yeah. Shower."

We're lying in bed, our arms and legs tangled together, and my thoughts running wild. My heart beats a mile a minute, and my hands are clammy. I know I just need to ask. We just need to rip off the Band-Aid. I take a deep breath.

"So, we need to talk."

He sighs. "I guess we do."

Seriously. Is that all he's going to give me here?

"I just want to know what it is we're doing," I say, sounding far more confident than I actually am. "I can handle whatever, but I just need to know. I'm thinking about it far too much."

I try a weak attempt at laughter.

"All I know is that I like you, Poppy. And my kids like you."

"I like you, too," I whisper. "And them."

"I have to tread carefully with stuff like this... because of them. I haven't dated anyone since my ex-wife. This is uncharted territory, and I can't pretend like I have it all figured out." He pushes his hand through my hair. "But I hate when you're not around. I think about you all the damn time."

"Yeah?" I can't help the grin that spreads across my face. I try to bite it back, I really do. The last thing I want to do is seem overly eager.

"Yeah." He laughs at my expression. "But I don't know what to tell the kids. Or, I guess, how to tell them. Or when? When do we decide that it's big enough to bring you into their life like that?"

I know he has a point, and I'm trying not to let it get to me that *that's* what he's hung up on after all the time I've spent with them over the last few weeks. They come see me at work every day and bring me breakfast. I've dyed their hair and picked flowers for Jolene. I've played video games with Wade and helped him with his reading. I've helped Rhett in the kitchen when he'll let me, and I've kind of melted into the rest of his family with weekend dinners and early morning cups of coffee.

It feels like I just…fit. So to hear that he's worried about whether or not we are serious enough to tell the kids hurts a little. But I have to remember they're not my kids, and I don't have any of my own. So I don't know what it's like to worry about bringing someone new into their lives. I haven't had the mother of my

BURNED   221

children up and leave one day just because she decided she didn't want this life anymore.

A sour feeling sits in my stomach at the thought. I don't understand parents who can leave their children like that.

"Poppy?" he asks, trying to get me to look at him. "Are you angry with me?"

"No," I assure him. "I will never be angry with you for taking care of your kids. I agree. We need to flesh this out a bit before we go involving them like that. But please know that I love them, and I would do anything for them."

"I know you do. I can see it in the way you are with them." He kisses me softly. "I love how much care and patience you have for them. Seeing them happy with you makes my chest ache. They deserve a woman like you in their life."

Now my chest aches, because that is the nicest damn thing Rhett Black has ever said to me. Scratch that. That is the nicest thing *anyone* has ever said to me.

"We'll take it as it goes. And maybe we'll just know when the time is right." I smile at him. "But you know what I think would be a really good start?"

He raises an eyebrow.

"You not being such a grumpy asshole all the time. Maybe start by cutting back on the grunting, and use your big-boy words instead."

He barks out a laugh and tucks me into his chest. I

breathe him in and listen to the deep rumble of his laughter through his rib cage.

"I can't make any promises there, poppyseed."

I just roll my eyes. Of course he can't. It's part of his damn DNA to grunt.

CHAPTER THIRTY-THREE

Rhett

"YOU'VE BEEN LESS grumpy these past few weeks," Hayes says as we watch the cattle mosey across the field to their new home.

I grunt.

"Wouldn't have anything to do with Poppy, would it?"

It has everything to do with Poppy. She comes over for dinners, and I sneak over to hers some afternoons before I go get the kids from Momma. I see her every day with my kids, teaching them how to train the dogs or taking them to see the new rescues. I've tried telling her that it's not her job to spend time with them or to watch them while Momma goes to town.

But she just ignores me, saying she has just as much fun as they do. And while I fought her on it at first, I've just started letting her do what she wants. Mainly because catching glimpses of them throughout the day makes my heart happy.

"Maybe."

"You lettin' her in?"

I glance at Hayes out of the corner of my eye. I don't want to answer that question. I'm letting her in as best I can, but I still have too much to worry about to let my guard down completely.

"Rhett, look." He sighs. "I know you hate this shit, but I want you to listen to me for once. Take it from someone who royally fucked up and wishes he could take it all back, yeah?"

When he doesn't continue, I realize he actually wants me to acknowledge him.

"I'm listening," I tell him.

"Good. I know you've been burned before. Leah really fucked you up—"

"Already heard all this from Wells," I say, cutting him off.

"Yeah, well, now you're gonna hear it from me, you stubborn asshole, because it doesn't seem to have sunk in." His horse takes a few steps and settles. His agitation is leaking into her. "You need to get over it. Let someone in who is good for you. Poppy is good for you. I've seen the way you look at her, like she lights everything up. And the way she treats your kids? Shit, man. You aren't gonna find that just anywhere."

"She's a whole decade younger than me."

"Get over the age thing," he groans. "Who gives a fuck?"

I huff. "People might. I don't want people talkin' about her or me or the kids. You know how this town is. Everyone is in everyone else's business, and she doesn't deserve having people talk about her behind her back for being with an old man. And my kids sure as shit don't deserve it."

"Take other people out of the equation. Because they aren't in your relationship. Do you, Rhett Black, really care that she's twenty-seven?"

"She's twenty-six."

"For literally like eight more days. Don't be an ass."

"I care that I would be saddlin' her with two young kids."

"She wants kids."

"How do you know that?" My brow furrows, and I can feel the anger in my chest start to build. Have they been talking? He's my brother, and it shouldn't bother me. But it does. I don't want anyone else getting close to her like that.

"Heard her chattin' with Momma about it last week, calm down. Momma asked her if she wanted kids some-day, and Poppy couldn't shut up about it."

I grunt again because I know that. She's told me herself she wants kids. So why am I so worried about the fact I have two? She clearly loves them and loves spending time with them. It's harder to get her to leave them at the end of the day than it is for her to leave me.

"I know." I sigh. "She's told me she wants kids. Multiple times. And I've seen her with Joey and Wade…she loves those fuckin' kids."

"She does," he agrees. "So what's really holding you back? *You* don't care that she's younger. You know she loves your kids. What else is there?"

I think about that question for a minute but come up blank. Is it that she technically works here? That should probably be something that makes me think twice, and it may have at first, but I don't really care anymore. It doesn't affect us like I thought it would.

Unfortunately, I think Hayes is right. Leah wanted this life until she decided the city had more to offer. And Poppy comes from a faster way of life. She's moved around so often it worries me that she can't put down roots. If I let her in and let her get close to my kids in that way and she decides she doesn't want this life anymore?

I can't do that to my kids.

"Alright, fine." We start to follow the cattle as the last of them are herded through the fence. "You're right. Leah fucked me up. She decided she didn't want kids anymore and didn't want this way of life. But this is who I am. Those kids are all I've got. And this ranch is in my blood. If I make that mistake again and let someone in who is just gonna walk away because they got a wild hair up their ass, the kids will get hurt."

"And you'll get hurt," he adds.

"Yeah."

"You're just gonna have to take a leap of faith with her. Trust her when she says this is what she wants. I mean, have you seen how much she loves this ranch? Sometimes I see her just lying on her back in the middle of a pasture, takin' in the sunshine."

"People do that shit at the beach all the time and then leave at the end of their vacation. Doesn't mean she wants to stay, Hayes."

"Have you asked her?" He leans forward, trying to get in my eyeline. I refuse to look at him. "You haven't, have you? You haven't asked her if she would want to stay?"

"For me? Or for the job?"

"For you, you ass." I can hear the frustration in his voice, and I don't blame him. I know I'm an ass. I know I'm difficult. Another reason why I'm worried she won't want to stay.

"Think it's a bit early to be askin' that sort of thing."

"Is it?" he asks. "Because from where I'm standing, she's falling for you, Rhett. I think she'd like to know if you are as well."

"When did you become the wise one?" I smirk over at him.

"I fucked up with River." He shrugs. "And ever

since, I've just had a lot of time to think on it. I don't want you to make the same mistake. You're my brother, and I love you. I want you to be happy, man."

"What happened with River, Hayes? You never said anything. She just stopped comin' around."

"We're talking about you."

I laugh. "Alright, then. But once my shit is sorted, I'm comin' for you."

"Mm," he hums. "You can try."

He kicks his horse into gear, and he's off, trotting down over the hill to catch up with the rest of the ranch hands and the cattle dogs. I stay behind, me and Lucille enjoying the sunset as it dips behind the mountains. The air gets cooler, and I know I need to head back. The kids are gonna wonder where I am if I'm late coming home.

"What do you think, Lucille? Should we head on home?" I pat her neck, and she snorts in response.

And then there's the picture in my mind of coming home not only to my kids but to Poppy as well. She wouldn't be living in that little cabin anymore. She'd be living with me. I could walk into my house and see her playing with the kids, their laughter filling the room. I would make us all dinner, and then we would both put the kids down before falling into bed together.

I think back to that night we left a dent in the drywall, and my cock stirs. I want that woman in my bed every goddamn night. I'm tired of sneaking her in after the kids are asleep or slinking off to her house in the afternoons when they won't miss us. I'm tired of hiding her — hiding that we're together.

Hayes is right. I'm going to have to trust her. I need to get over my shit and take that risk with her. I sigh and direct Lucille back toward Momma's house so I can pick up the kids and head home. I'll talk to Poppy after the adoption event. Maybe at the birthday party Momma is throwin' for her. I'll need a drink or two in me to work up the courage anyway.

Because if she says no…I think she might break my damn heart.

CHAPTER THIRTY-FOUR

Poppy

BETTY IS FINALLY COMING out of her shell again. It's been long days, and some nights, spent sitting with her, but she's finally starting to crawl back out of her little home to eat. She's even let me put her on a lead again so she can potty outside instead of in her room. She's still startled easily when she hears the kids running around, but she's getting better. Less flinching and no more hackles raised.

She lies next to me on the floor now, her head resting peacefully on my thigh. With slow, deliberate movements, I pet the top of her head and twirl her soft ears between my fingers. She snores and then opens her eyes when Wells slowly walks over to us. Sweet Betty is used to him by now and lets him sit down opposite me.

"Ready for the event this weekend?"

"The adoption or the birthday party?" I joke,

knowing that whatever his mom has planned is most certainly an event. She's been talking about it for weeks.

"The adoption." He laughs.

"I've been meaning to ask you about that. Since this is where we're having the event, don't you think Betty would feel better somewhere else?"

I've been thinking about this ever since he told me about the event. How is she supposed to relax with all the noise? The new sights, smells, and sounds are going to be terrifying for her. I'd rather her be off-site somewhere, maybe even in my little house.

"Yeah, I guess you're right. We could put her in another barn. Although, the smell of the other animals and the unfamiliarity might make her anxious."

I sigh. I never thought about that. Even if I took her over to mine that day, there's still the chance she could be just as uncomfortable.

"What if I start taking her over to mine?" I ask. "I could start first thing tomorrow. Tonight, I can go into town and get the stuff I would need, and then over the next few days, we can get her accustomed to my place."

"You want to adopt her?" His eyes go wide.

I would love to adopt her, but Rhett and the kids are in the back of my mind. Betty needs someone that can care for her and only her. I would always be nervous about the kids, and while I know Betty was only scared when she bit me, I don't know when she'll be scared again. The responsible thing to do is find someone who fits her needs better than I do.

"Not adopt," I reluctantly say. "Just keep her safe and calm from now through the event. Keep her comfortable."

"Fine by me," he says. "Just be careful. If you get hurt again, Rhett might lose his goddamn mind."

I snort and roll my eyes. "He's such a worrier."

"Having two kids on your own will do that." He rests his head back on the wall. "On top of having to take care of all of us as kids...and as adults."

"You mean Dean?" I ask, figuring that's what he means by taking care of them as adults. Because Wells seems to have his life mostly together, and while Hayes can slack off, he's still a fully functioning human. But I haven't heard much about Dean, and I'm guessing he's the one causing the extra stress.

He hums and nods. "A lot of that fell on Rhett. Dad tried at first, but when Rhett took over the ranch, it had to be him that fronted the money for all of Dean's failed rehabs."

"That has to be hard." I reach out and give his hand a quick squeeze. "I grew up in a small town where almost everyone was addicted to something at some point in their life. It was never a family member, but I had friends. That was hard to watch."

"We never thought it was an issue when Dean was younger because we were all drinking and partying. It felt normal." He shrugs. "But then he started grabbing a beer before heading out on the ranch...at six in the morning."

I wince.

"Yeah." He groans. "We should've known then. But we just kept making excuses for him. And when we'd go out, he would drink *so much*, Poppy. Like, if it had been any of us, we would've been on the floor. But it's like his tolerance was just so incredibly high."

"How'd you decide enough was enough?"

"Yeah, that's not a pleasant story." His head falls forward into his hands, and he rubs them down his face. "The first time we realized something was seriously wrong was when he got drunk and yelled at Momma. And I mean *yelled*. He came over for Saturday dinner and went to get a drink. Momma had emptied out the entire house of alcohol. I guess she knew something was wrong before we did. He fucking lost it on her."

I can't imagine anyone yelling at Katherine. It breaks my heart to think about her own son screaming at her over throwing out the alcohol.

"Rhett had to drag his ass outside. The next day, Dean started going to AA meetings. He did pretty good, at first." Wells' face has the saddest expression, and it just breaks my heart. "He got a few chips under his belt before he relapsed. We should've expected it, honestly. But Addie's death hit us all hard, and it was difficult enough to take care of ourselves, let alone the functioning alcoholic."

"Oh, Wells."

He gives me a weak smile.

"Anyway, after a few months of that, we got him into a short-term care facility. On Rhett's dime, obviously. He came back a new man. He looked healthier and seemed so much happier."

"He fell off again?" I ask, assuming that's where we're headed.

He nods. "Didn't even last a month. Pops kicked him out. And I mean out. He wasn't allowed within a hundred feet of the ranch for years. He never even knew Rhett and Leah got married. He wasn't here for Jo or Wade being born. Dean was just…gone."

"Where'd he go?"

Wells shrugs. "No clue. He just showed up one night, beggin' for forgiveness. It was pouring rain, and Momma couldn't stand to let him just freeze to death. She convinced Pops to let him in, and for months, she babied him and tried to help. Rhett spent thousands on therapy and in-home visits with addiction counselors.

"About three months ago," he continues, "Rhett shipped him off to some fancy long-term in-patient rehab in Colorado. I know it has to be expensive. And I know that's why the ranch is struggling. He's sank so much money into Dean that he's barely keeping his head above water on anything else."

"Three months ago… Shouldn't he be coming back soon?"

Wells nods. "Rhett paid for six months. Said the last time he did ninety days, it didn't do shit. He was getting six months of therapy and rehab before he was allowed to step a boot back on this ranch."

"I can't imagine the amount of stress." I play with Betty's ears between my fingers and try to think of what to say. What can anyone say? "So not only does Rhett have his kids and his ranch to worry about, he's also worrying about Dean."

"Every damn day. I know Dean is on his mind constantly."

"Why hasn't he said anything?"

"Who knows, city slicker." He winks at me, his playful side coming back. "Probably because he doesn't want to scare you off."

"He couldn't scare me off if he tried. Pretty sure he was trying there for a while."

That gets a good laugh from Wells.

"Yeah, I think he was, too. But only because you scared the shit out of him." Betty gets up and slowly moves over to Wells, sniffing his pant leg before lying down next to him instead.

"I scared the shit out of him? He was the grumpy one! He was such an asshole."

"Yeah," he says, laughing. "He was. But that's just Rhett. And you're the first girl that's made him do a double take since the divorce. He's never dated, never slept around, never even *looked* at another woman 'til you popped into the picture."

My ego and my heart inflate.

"Yeah?"

"Okay, don't go lettin' it get to your head," he teases. "Keep bein' good to him. He'll get his head out of his ass one of these days."

"I know you aren't talkin' about me." Rhett's voice comes from the front of the barn, and when I look up, I'm greeted with the lovely sight of his strong body leaning against the doorframe. The sun's behind him, outlining his muscles and cowboy hat. He's a wet dream come to life.

"Would never dream of it, brother," Wells says, slowly getting up. Betty walks back to her bed in the corner and plops down with a huff. "Good talk, city slicker."

Rhett walks through the barn, and Wells meets him halfway, stopping him to whisper something in his ear before patting him on the back and sending him my way.

"Rude to whisper!" I shout after Wells. He just waves his hand and leaves.

"Hey," Rhett says once he's next to me. His eyes drink me in, and that sweet smile he tends to reserve only for me is gracing his full lips.

"Hi."

"Came by to see if you wanted to have dinner with me tonight."

Butterflies explode in my stomach.

"Like a date?" I ask.

He chuckles. "Yeah, poppyseed. Like a date."

"You taking me out for a night on the town, Rhett Black? Want me all to yourself?"

He takes my hand and pulls me up off the floor and right into his arms. His face is immediately hovering over mine as his hands grab onto my ass.

"I always want you all to myself, Poppy Sharpe." He kisses me so hard I think I start to see stars.

"Well, alright, cowboy. All you had to do was ask."

CHAPTER THIRTY-FIVE

Rhett

THE KIDS ARE with my parents until I get back, so I drive straight across the fields to her little house that's tucked away against the tree line. She seems to really like it here. When she was staying with me, she was gushing about the style of the kitchen. Maybe if she moves in, she can put her own personal touch on my kitchen.

God knows it needs it. That whole house has fallen into a white-and-grey theme. I just don't know how to put my own stamp on it, and Leah never cared to. Not that she was there long enough to do anything. It was finished being built right as Wade was born, and she left soon after.

"Hey, cowboy!"

Poppy's voice breaks through my thoughts, and when I see her jog down the steps and out to my truck, my brain goes completely blank. Her hair is still vibrant, and she's curled it into subtle waves. She's wearing a sundress with those cowboy boots she bought recently. I hope she's got thick socks on because those suckers are gonna tear her feet to bits if she doesn't.

I jump out and run around the truck. A gentleman never lets a woman open her own door. One of those cute little eyebrows raises up as she eyes me.

"I can open my own door, you know."

"I know, poppyseed. I'm just tryin' to be nice." She grins as I wait impatiently for her to get in. "Well?"

"Aren't you going to tell me I look nice?" She does a little twirl, making the hem of her dress fly up around the tops of her thighs.

I reach out and grab her, pulling her tight to my body as I kiss her hard. I've missed her today, and seein' her all dressed up has my chest aching. She grunts but leans into me, opening her mouth as my tongue slips in. And then she's grabbing the cowboy hat off my head and placing it on her own.

Fuck, she looks cute.

"Completes the look, right?" Her smile is wide, and the setting sun makes her eyes almost glow.

I lean in and kiss her cheek. "I'm gonna fuck you with nothin' but those boots and my hat on later."

"Promises, promises, Rhett Black."

Before she can stop me, I grab her around the waist and lift her into the truck. She tries to hand my hat back to me, but I like it better on her. Plus, when people see her with me, they're gonna know it's mine. Which means they'll know that *she* is mine. And while we haven't fully confirmed that yet, I plan to tonight.

———————————◆

I take her to a little spot in town that's half bar and half restaurant. We don't have time to go next door to the bigger city, where there are much fancier places to eat. I want to give her the best, but I can't leave the kids with Momma and Pops all night. If I want to have dinner, get her home and naked, and then pick up my kids before bedtime, we are gonna have to keep it short.

"This is so cute," she says, smiling at everyone we walk past to get to our booth. She slides in first, and I take the side opposite. We put our drink orders in, and she immediately asks for an appetizer of fried pickles. She hadn't even looked at the menu, but luckily, they have them here.

"Do you like it here, Poppy?"

She looks up from her Dr. Pepper with wide eyes and takes the hat off like she means business.

"By here, you mean Cane Creek? Or the restaurant?"

"Cane Creek. Well, both? I guess?"

God, I sound like an idiot. My nerves have my palms sweating and my mind racin'. I can barely focus on anything other than how fucking good she looks in that dress.

"I love it," she says with a sigh, letting my muscles relax. "I came here because I wanted a change. I grew up in a small town, and ever since, I've just been hopping from one big city to another. Suddenly, I thought maybe I don't feel settled because a big city isn't where I'm supposed to be."

She shrugs and sips from her straw.

"So, if we were to continue this," I say, gesturing back and forth between us, "you wouldn't feel like I was keeping you somewhere you didn't want to be?"

Those pretty cheeks flush a dark pink, and she struggles to make eye contact. Now I'm really wishing I had sat next to her because I could grab that little chin and force her to look up at me.

"No, Rhett," she finally says. "You wouldn't be holding me hostage."

The pickles come out, and we place the rest of our order. One good thing about living in a small town is the restaurant service is impeccably fast. She dips the little pickle chip in ranch, absolutely slathering it with the dressing, and then pops it in her mouth.

I will not let that turn me on. I will not let that turn me on.

"Poppy." She looks up at me and smiles, waiting for

me to continue. Jesus Christ, I'm in love with this woman. "I'd like to tell the kids."

The biggest, sweetest smile spreads across her lips, and I almost reach across to kiss her.

"Yeah?" She tucks a piece of hair behind her ear.

"Yeah. What do you think?"

"Rhett, I would love that. I would love to tell them. If you're sure you're all ready for that."

"I've watched you with them every day since you got here. They're almost obsessed with you, and you treat them like your own. There's nothing more I could ask for from a partner." I take a deep breath, knowing that once we tell them, there's no going back. That cat will be out of the bag, and we'll have to deal with any consequences that come with it. "We should tell them."

She squeals, slides out of her seat, and throws herself into mine. She wraps me in her arms and kisses me hard on the cheek. Now it's my turn to blush because she just got everyone's attention in this damn restaurant, and I have never been a fan of PDA.

"People are lookin', woman." I half-heartedly scold her and then kiss her back.

"Let 'em look. It's about time people know I'm yours, right?" She winks at me and then settles against me, her head leanin' on my shoulder as she continues to munch on the basket of pickles.

The rest of the date goes by quickly. I think we're both ready for me to make good on my promise from earlier because while we have a conversation and joke around, we both eat our meals in record time. The waitress puts our bill down, and I pay in cash, tipping her well before Poppy grabs my hat and we practically run out the front door.

"You have time to fuck me in these cowgirl boots before you have to get the kids?" she asks, spinning around to face me as I cage her in against the passenger-side door of my truck. She bites her lip and smiles as she glances down at my jeans, seeing that I'm already hard as a damn rock for her.

What can I say? Seeing Poppy in my hat does something to me.

"Poppy," I growl against her neck, kissing my way up to her jaw. I know we're out in the middle of a parking lot where anyone could see us, but I'm a man possessed. I don't give a fuck. Let them watch. "What are you doin' to me?"

"Same thing you're doing to me, cowboy. Making it hard to breathe."

I run my hands up her thighs until they're under the soft fabric of her dress. Her breath hitches, and I go higher. She's not wearing any fucking panties. I slip a hand between her thighs, dipping a finger into her slit. My girl is already so wet for me...I'm tempted to turn her around and fuck her against this damn truck.

"No panties?" I ask.

She shakes her head and kisses me, biting my lower lip as she pulls away.

"I wasn't sure if we'd need to make it a quickie in the truck." She grins, and it's full of so many wicked promises. "I wanted to be prepared."

"Bad girl, Poppy." I smack the side of her ass.

"Whoops." She shrugs, all attitude.

"What am I going to do with you?" I kiss her again, my fingertips digging into her ass as I press us tighter against the truck.

"Hopefully rip my dress off and fuck me until I can't walk?"

"Jesus Christ, Poppy Sharpe. That mouth..."

"Get in the truck, and I'll show you exactly what my mouth can do."

I may be just a simple country boy, but I'm no idiot. When a woman says something like that, you get your ass in the damn truck. So after I lift her in, barely registering her sweet laugh as I do so, I run around the damn thing to jump in with the eagerness of a schoolboy.

Let's get this damn show on the road.

CHAPTER THIRTY-SIX

Rhett

THANK god for old trucks and bench seats. Her mouth has been around my cock the entire drive home, but I refuse to finish in her mouth. The bumps in the driveway as we drive over to her house make my cock slip deep into her throat. She coughs, caught by surprise, and I damn near break my steering wheel in two.

By the time we park in front of her house, I'm losing all control. We aren't going to make it inside. I need her now. Yanking her off my dick, I pull her mouth to mine, kissing her hard as she crawls on top of me. She straddles me, her thick thighs squeezing my hips as her bare center makes contact with my cock.

"Poppy," I groan. "You gonna be mad if I rip this dress?" I kiss down her neck, and she arches against me. "Because I need you now, baby. I can't wait any longer, and I really liked the idea of you in nothin' but these boots and my hat."

"Just shut up and rip it already." She barely gets the words out before the sound of fabric tearing fills the cab. That pretty little dress tears so easily, and she shimmies the rest of the way out of it.

"God, you're fucking perfect." I push her back and lean forward, desperate to taste her skin. Her pink nipples are hard, and I tease them with the tip of my tongue. She lets out the sweetest mewling noises while grinding down onto me.

"I need you inside of me, Rhett."

"You're in control, poppyseed. Take what you want."

She shifts up on her knees, honking the horn in the process. I laugh into her mouth as I kiss her again and again. I can't get enough, and as she lines me up and begins to let gravity do all the work, I'm fucking lost. My hands grab hold of her hips, and I thrust up into her, not able to wait any longer.

Her mouth forms an O, and our breath mingles. We just sit for a moment, staring at each other while she acclimates to my size. The windows of the truck fog up, and her hand slams against the one on my side as I begin to move inside of her. Her tits bounce, and her soft belly presses against my own.

"God, you feel so good." Her other hand holds my hat onto her head as I fuck her from underneath.

I like this view.

"That's right, poppyseed. Ride me. Ride this fat cock until you're coming all over it." She moans my name, making my fingertips dig even harder into her flesh as I pull her down to meet each thrust. "This cunt is squeezing me so tight."

"Fuck, that mouth," she groans.

"You like my mouth, Poppy? You like it when I talk dirty to you?"

"Yes." She hisses through her teeth.

"Are you *my* little slut, Poppy? Does this pussy come only for me? Only for my cock?"

"Yes, yes, yes," she chants. She's getting close.

"Tell me, baby. Tell me how this pussy belongs to me now." I lick my thumb and press it firmly on her clit, making her give me the sweetest fucking whimpers.

"It's yours," she pants, and her hands settle around the back of my neck, her fingers tangling in my hair. "It's all yours, cowboy."

Her eyes bore into my own, and I can't stop the flood of emotions from breaking free. We pour everything we haven't said yet into our kiss. Our tongues dance together, and she begins to grind against me as I thrust deep inside.

"I'm gonna come, Rhett."

She bites her pretty bottom lip and throws her head back. It gives me the most delicious view of her entire body, all soft curves and flushed from the exertion. I keep circling her clit, praying to god she comes before I do. I deserve a goddamn medal for holding out when I have this woman bouncing on top of me.

"That's right. Come for me, Poppy. Show me how a woman rides her man."

Her orgasm rips through her, and it triggers my own almost immediately. She milks me for all I'm fuckin' worth as she grinds down onto me. Poppy pulls me in, pressing my face to her chest as her heart damn near beats out of her chest. I'm sure mine is doin' the same because I can see stars every time I blink.

"Fuck." She laughs and kisses my sweaty forehead. "Now I have to walk naked into my house."

I run my hands down her legs and over those sexy fucking cowgirl boots she's wearin'. My hat is still on her head, albeit a bit crooked from all the bouncing she just did. She looks sexy as hell.

"That's the good thing about livin' on a ranch," I tell her, kissing those soft and swollen lips. "No one's gonna see a damn thing."

She looks around, realizing we are completely alone in the middle of nowhere, with only the moon lighting up her path.

"What if one of your brothers just so happens to come over to visit?"

"Then I'll gouge their eyes out."

"Rhett!" Her laughter fills the truck. It's musical and free, and I eat it up.

"I will, Poppy," I growl and lick her neck. "You're all mine. Which means no one else gets to look. And if they do? I kick their ass."

She moans. "What does it say about me that those words turn me on?"

I chuckle against the pulse point in her throat. It's beating against my lips like a hummingbird.

"It means you're perfect for me. And you like being mine."

She leans into me, resting her head on my shoulder as we come down from the high. I just hold her, relishing every second I get of this. Because while I know we said we're gonna tell the kids, and that inevitably means she's considering stayin', I can't help but wonder if she actually will. And I don't want to miss a moment of this.

"We steamed up your truck like Jack and Rose." She laughs softly and draws a heart on the window. In the center, she draws an *R* and a *P*.

"Momma and Pops carved their initials like that into a tree at the back of the property," I tell her. "They picked one of the oldest oaks, and Pops took his knife out to carve their initials in a heart. He proposed in front of that tree, and they got married in front of that tree. Momma even told him she was pregnant with me in front of that damn tree."

"That's the sweetest fucking thing I've ever heard." Her eyes are wet when she looks at me. "They really love each other. You're so lucky to have had that…a picture of what real love looks like. Something to strive for, you know?"

"Guess I never thought of it like that."

"You took it for granted." She smiles and kisses my nose. "I probably would've, too, if it were the norm in my house. All that love all the time."

"You want that kind of love, Poppy? That carve your initials in a tree type love?"

"Of course I do." She rests her arms on my shoulders and plays with my hair. "I want that love. I want the babies. I want grey hair and rocking chairs. All that boring stuff. Don't you?"

I grunt out a laugh and avoid the question. I'm not ready to answer that just yet.

"Kids are anything but boring, sweet girl."

Her smile falters, and fuck if I don't regret not answering.

"Speaking of." She sighs. "You have a couple of them that are patiently waiting for their daddy to get home."

"Poppy—"

"Hand me my dress?" She gives me a weak smile. "Or what's left of it, I guess."

I give in and hand it to her. No sense in trying to backtrack now, especially since she's right. I do have two kids at Momma's house, and I haven't seen them all day. Even though I don't want to leave Poppy, and I definitely don't want to leave her like this, I *do* want to see my kids.

She slips off my rapidly deflating cock and tucks part of her dress between her thighs and covers the front of her with the rest. Holding it up with one hand, she takes my hat off with the other.

"Keep it."

"I'm not keeping your hat. Don't be silly."

But I just stare at her because I don't want it. I want to see her in it. I want to see if she'll wear it around the ranch while she works or if I'll come over and catch her wearin' it around her house.

She sighs and pops it back on her head. "Fine. But it looks better on you."

"Not a chance, sweetheart."

Before I can tell her good night, she's out of the truck and shuttin' the door, effectively ending our conversation and date. It went really fuckin' well until it didn't. I always seem to do that — ruin perfectly good things. But like Poppy said, I'm a grumpy asshole. And I guess that tends to come with the territory.

I just wish it didn't hurt her in the process.

CHAPTER THIRTY-SEVEN

Poppy

IT FEELS weird to sit down and tell the kids we're giving this a go when we left things not so great last night. But we agreed to tell them, and I don't want to take a step back, even if that might be the healthier thing to do. Instead, I'm going full steam ahead here.

"This seems serious," Jolene says, looking back and forth between me and her daddy.

We're at Rhett's place, and both kids are sitting on the living room couch while we stand in front of them. I didn't want to do it like we were having some sort of committee hearing, but Rhett didn't know how else to do it. So here we are.

Jolene's comment makes Wade nervous, and his little eyes anxiously look over at his sister.

"It is serious," Rhett says, all gruff and crossing his

arms. What in the world is he doing? Suddenly, it's like he's having the birds and the bees talk to two teenagers.

I nudge him and give him a look, trying to tell him to lighten the fuck up.

"Okay, it's not *that* serious."

He bends down to their level, and thankful he's done so, I follow. I plop down on my butt and scoot closer to both of them, smiling hopefully. I'm so nervous. I'm terrified they're going to freak out, and then Rhett will have no choice but to break things off. And then how fucking awkward will that be? I'll have to move. There is no way in hell that we break up and I can just go back to normal like nothing happened. No way. Ha ha. No, sir.

"What's goin' on?" Wade asks, pulling his comfort blanket up to his nose. He loves the smell of that dirty old thing. But I had something similar, so I can't really judge.

"So, you guys like Poppy, right?"

Jolene and Wade both nod.

"She takes me to see my cow," Jolene says, giggling like it's a secret she isn't supposed to tell.

"And she helped me learn how to spell things," Wade adds. "And my hair is purple!"

Rhett laughs, that soft, quiet laugh he reserves for them. It's one I got to hear so many times when I was staying here while I recovered. It's a laugh that's full of love and wonder, like he can't believe how lucky he is that these two kids are his.

"Well, I really like Poppy, too."

"Yeah?" Jolene's eyes light up. "*Like* like?"

"Yes, baby girl. I *like* like Poppy."

"And she likes you?" Jolene sounds shocked, and I can't help but snort. That girl has so much of her daddy's attitude.

Rhett turns and looks at me, his eyebrow raised.

"I do," I say, getting my laughter under control. "I like him a lot. And I was wondering if it would be okay if I started spending some more time over here?"

"Sleepovers!" Wade shouts as he throws his arms up to the sky, his blanket following and whacking him in the face.

"If that's okay with you…" Rhett places a hand on each of their knees, getting a little more serious. "I want you to know that both of you will always come first."

"Always," I agree. "No matter what."

"Daddy, why would we care?" Jolene asks. "You're sad all the time. But when Poppy is here, you smile more."

That cracks my heart in two. I feel it physically crack wide freaking open. My chest aches, and my hand goes to Rhett's arm, giving it two little squeezes. I make him smile.

"And she plays games with us. Do you promise

you'll still play games?" Wade asks, turning to face me. "You won't spend all your time with Daddy, right?"

"I will play all the games you want."

"Poppy," Jolene says, her voice a bit quiet. "Does this mean you like us, too?"

"Of course I do!" I tell her, fighting back the tears that are threatening to fall. "I like you far more than your grumpy daddy." I wink at her, making her laugh before I pull them both in for a hug.

"Maybe," Wade whispers when I hug them, "you could be like our mommy or something?"

Oh, god. Oh, god.

If my heart cracked in half earlier, it has been fucking obliterated now. I can't hold back the tears. They come hot and fast and soak my face. I squeeze both of them tighter as Rhett's hand comes up to rub comforting circles on my back.

I didn't come here for this. I didn't move to a random town in the middle of nowhere to start a life with someone and his two kids. But that's what has happened, and I don't find myself regretting a single moment. Rhett crashed into my life at a time when I wanted a home. And he brought his two kids with him. They've worked their way into my heart, and I can't see myself letting them leave it.

"I would be honored to be whatever it is you need me to be," I tell them, pulling away so that I can look them both in their eyes. "Anything you need, that's what I am."

Jolene wipes the tears from my face, and I laugh at how grown-up she's acting with all of this. Both Rhett and I were worried that this might not go over well or that it would be too much for them to understand. But it seems they understand perfectly fine, and they're ready and willing to let me come into their lives.

"I think we should do something fun," Jolene announces, nodding her head once like she has decided it is time to move on from all this seriousness.

"Oh, yeah?" Rhett smiles at her and pulls Wade into his lap. The blanket follows. "What would you like to do, baby girl?"

A wicked little grin spreads across her lips, and she looks like she is up to no good. Ornery little thing.

"I say we go make s'mores!" she shouts triumphantly.

"Baby," Rhett groans. "That means I'm gonna have to make a fire."

I turn to look at him.

"Are you telling me that you, Rhett Black, a cowboy, don't want to go make a fire for his baby girl? For s'mores?"

"Yeah, Daddy!" Wade says, joining our side of the team. "What gives?"

"What gives?" Rhett laughs, and his tone is shocked.

"Good lord, son. You're spending far too much time with your Uncle Hayes. You're soundin' just like him."

"Don't change the subject." Jolene points a sassy little finger at her daddy. "Please, Daddy?"

"Please, Daddy?" I ask, teasing him with a sickly sweet voice.

"I'll make the fire if you promise to never call me that again." He snorts and gives me a playful shove that leaves me cackling.

"Fine, fine," I concede. "You go get the fire going, and we'll get all the ingredients."

"Startin' to regret this already," he mumbles as he helps me up off the floor. "All three of you are gonna be gangin' up on me, aren't you?"

"Only when it comes to s'mores." I grin up at him, and he kisses me. Nothing but a quick peck on the lips. But the kids think it's hilarious and start hollering as they run around us.

"They're kissin'!" Jolene shouts as Wade pretends to gag.

Rhett was right — kids are anything but boring. And damn did my life need some fun.

CHAPTER THIRTY-EIGHT

Poppy

BETTY IS all set up in her crate with blankets and toys. I've also given her a couple of calming treats to make sure she can get some sleep while I'm gone. I'll run back halfway through the day to check on her, but it's still going to be a lot longer than she's used to going without seeing someone.

I have nervous jitters. I've worked really hard with these dogs to make sure they're trained and happy and well-fed. I've given them everything they need to hopefully find good homes. Wells says we will have loads of people coming in from all the surrounding towns since it's one of the biggest events in the area.

Throwing on Rhett's cowboy hat, I walk out the front, only to be greeted by my handsome man sitting up high on Lucille. Good god, he looks good up there, his Wranglers stretching tight against his muscled thighs and his strong forearms flexing as he holds the reins.

"Lookin' mighty good in that hat, poppyseed."

I show off the whole outfit, the dirt under my boots crunching as I spin in place. I know I have his favorite pair of jeans on, and I'm rewarded when his eyes linger all over my body when I face him again. And they don't stop as I saunter over to him.

"I didn't know we'd be taking Lucille." I run my hand through her soft mane.

"Come here." His hand reaches out for me, and I take it as I shove my foot in the stirrup. Rhett tugs me up, and I throw a leg over Lucille, settling in against his back. He smells woodsy like his bodywash, and I can't help but take a deep breath with my nose pressed between his shoulder blades.

"Get a good whiff?"

"Mhm," I hum against him.

"I showered."

"I can smell."

He laughs at my gentle ribbing. I'm nervous and excited all at the same time, so I take some of that out by poking fun at Rhett.

"Happy birthday, Poppy." He looks at me over his shoulder, and I wrap my arms around his center, hugging him tight.

"Thank you." My chin sits on his shoulder.

"I was going to bring you somethin', but the kids

really wanted to be with us when I gave it to you. They helped me pick it out. Is tonight okay?"

"You didn't have to get me anything." But my heart flutters all the same.

"I wanted to." One of his hands runs over my forearms, leaving goose bumps where his calluses scratch my skin. I love his hands, worn and tough from the constant manual labor. The way they handle my body is such a turn-on. "Ready to go?"

"Giddyup, cowboy."

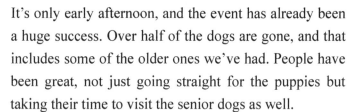

It's only early afternoon, and the event has already been a huge success. Over half of the dogs are gone, and that includes some of the older ones we've had. People have been great, not just going straight for the puppies but taking their time to visit the senior dogs as well.

And they all behave so well, not jumping too much on anyone and showing off all the tricks I've taught them. I've been able to talk to every person who has adopted, going over their application and making sure they're the right fit for the dog they wanted. It's been great meeting so many people from the area. I feel like they're welcoming me into this life, and it helps my confidence when it comes to staying here for good.

If that's what Rhett wants.

"Hey, Poppy!" Wells calls me over as I walk back from letting Betty out for a break.

He's standing next to a girl who looks a little familiar, like I've seen her before. Her hair is so black it almost looks blue or purple, like an oil spill. Legs for days and tattoos down her arms, she looks like the cool girl I always wanted to be in high school.

"Poppy, this is River," Wells introduces us. "River, Poppy."

"Hi!" I shake her hand. "It's so nice to meet you."

"Nice to meet you, too." She smiles, but she looks so nervous. Her blue eyes keep darting around like she's looking for someone. "I've heard a lot about you from Wells here. He was telling me that you have one you've been working with a lot that's been…struggling?"

"Betty, yeah. She was a scared little thing when I first started working with her. And we did have a little setback a few weeks ago. She got scared, she bit me, and…yeah. Anyway, we've bounced back, and she's doing much better."

"River's been bugging me for the past year to find her a dog," Wells says, and I realize now that River might actually *want* Betty.

"And he's always saying that he won't help me unless I come by. Well, here I am." She nudges him with her shoulder. "I was wondering if I could meet her, maybe?"

Emotion clogs my throat. It's hard to not view Betty as mine. But if Wells trusts River, and he must because he wouldn't bring just anyone to meet Betty, then I can trust her, too. And Betty deserves someone who can give her all the love and the proper environment to grow in.

"Yeah!" I clear my voice, trying to swallow back the tears. "I would love for you to meet her. She's still very shy of new people, so we would have to introduce you slowly. If you're interested, I think it would be best for us to keep her here for a while and you come visit her daily and sit with her. I can kind of show you and tell you what I've done to gain her trust."

"River works at the vet's office in town—"

"And I bartend at night," she interrupts. "I'm not, like, a veterinarian or anything. I'm just a technician."

"That's still important. You work with dogs every day, and you know how to love and handle the ones who need a little extra care." Wells puts a hand on her shoulder, giving it a light squeeze. I wonder if there's something going on between the two of them, but he lets go quickly, and she keeps looking around.

Maybe she's looking for another brother? I try to subtly look at the crowd to find who it is she's seeking out, but the only other brother that's here is Rhett, skulking in the corner. My grumpy cowboy is trying his hardest to avoid talking to anyone. He catches my gaze and winks in my direction. Always watching over me.

"That's perfect." I turn back to River with a smile. "She's over at the house I'm staying in. I figured today might be too much for her with all the noise and such. I can take you over there now, and we can—"

"Poppy!"

My blood runs hot and cold at the same time. I know that voice. It's a voice I thought I left behind when I moved here.

Wells and River both look at the person behind me, and I can see Rhett behind them, looking as well. His face is set in a scowl as he stares, and even though he has no clue who that person is, he does know that there is a man calling my name. And he does not like it.

"Poppy! Hey!" In one fell swoop, Ethan's arms are around me and lifting my body off the ground.

"Oh, shit," I hear Wells murmur.

"Happy birthday, princess!"

I'm too stunned to speak. I just stand there like a fish, my mouth opening and closing because I can't find the fucking words. Why in the hell is he here?

"Uh, Poppy?" Wells asks, scooting in closer. River takes a step back. "You wanna introduce us to your *friend* here?"

The emphasis on the word "friend" reminds me that Rhett is here. Oh, god. Rhett is watching.

"Hey, name's Ethan," he says, outstretching his hand to Wells. But Wells just looks at it until Ethan lets his hand drop back to his side. "I figured I'd come see

Poppy for her birthday. See if she's ready to head back
to the city with me yet." Ethan laughs and wraps his arm
around my shoulder, pulling me into his body. "I'm
shocked she's made it this long!"

I want to throw up. I want to scream. But I can't
fucking speak. My voice is just gone as I look up at him,
then to Wade, and then to the corner where Rhett is
standing. His whole body is vibrating with anger,
kicking my brain back into a functioning state.

I pull away from Ethan's grasp and lean in, whis-
pering with as much venom as I can.

"Can we speak outside, please?"

Ethan looks genuinely confused, although why, I'm
not sure. I was very, very confident that I ended this. I
walked away; I told him I was *not* coming back. And I
told him that we were over. Done with.

Rhett storms out, the woodsy scent of him reaching
me as he brushes past me.

"Rhett, wait!" I run after him, grabbing his arm just
as he makes it out the doors.

"No, Poppy. You are nothin' but a city girl who's
come here for a summer vacation." His words are spat
out with so much anger my throat closes up. "You don't
have to pretend you're here for more than that anymore.
But you *definitely* don't get to break my kids' hearts in
the process. I'll be happy to see you go at the end of
your contract."

"You're a bad liar, Rhett Black," I choke out. "You

don't get to pretend you don't feel this. And you definitely don't get to dismiss the love I have for your kids." I press my finger into his chest, speaking low so only he can hear. "The only reason you'd be happy to watch me go is so you can ogle my ass on the way out."

Such a stupid thing to say, and petty, bringing this whole thing between us down to sex when it's not. It's so much more than that. But anger has eliminated the filter between my brain and my mouth.

"Go home, Poppy." He grits it out between his teeth like he can't bear to actually say it.

"Talk to me."

"No. Go home. I've seen enough."

"You've seen nothing! You saw a huge misunderstanding. Ethan—"

"Poppy," he growls, his entire body flexing into hard muscle. A vein pops in his neck, and his fists clench as he looms over me. All of his handsome features are transformed by anger and hurt.

"Rhett." I choke out his name like a sob. I reach out, but he pulls away.

"Go. Home."

He walks away but turns back after a few steps. Hope soars in my chest. Maybe he's going to hear me out, give me a chance to explain.

"And take my fuckin' hat off."

CHAPTER THIRTY-NINE

Poppy

"WHAT THE HELL WAS HAPPENING THERE?" Ethan's voice creeps over me like big angry vines.

"What the hell are you doing here?" I spin around, grabbing his arm, and yank him out of the view of everyone else. Because everyone is staring, thanks to Rhett's tantrum.

"I came to surprise you. I know when you left, you said you didn't want anything long-distance, but I figured it's been over a month now…you must be getting bored…?" He trails off when he sees just how angry I am. I can feel it vibrating off me.

"You had no right, Ethan. We broke up. We are not together. You don't get to just show up and act like you're here to take me 'home.'" I use little finger quotes on the word "home" because it's not home for me anymore.

This is home for me. Rhett is my home.

"Okay, you're overreacting." He rolls his eyes and crosses his arms across his chest. "How was I supposed to know you'd already jumped into bed with someone else?"

"Excuse me?" I almost shout. "One, you wouldn't know what I was doing here because we are broken up. There is a reason I have not spoken to you since I left. Fuck, you're delusional. And second, what I do in my life now is none of your fucking business. I don't owe you any explanations of what I choose to do with my time."

"Jesus Christ, Poppy." His face turns disgusted. "Since when did you become such a bitch? Are your daddy issues rooted so deep that you decided to fuck one?"

"Alright, bud. Probably time for you to go," Wells says, walking up next to us while I just gape at Ethan. Did he *really* just say that? To my face? Wells places a friendly hand on my shoulder, and River hovers at the barn doors, probably wondering what the fuck she walked into today.

"It is," I agree. "Go home. Do not contact me. Do not think about me. Keep my name out of your fucking mouth."

Am I being a little harsh? Maybe. I can't decide if my response is fully warranted or not, but I also don't really care. I'm so angry over what he's done to my relationship with Rhett that it's blinding me to every-thing else.

"Happily," Ethan states. "Have fun fucking the old man. I'm sure his stamina is top-notch." Sarcasm just drips from his fucking tone.

What is it about men that makes them so petty and gross when their pride is hurt?

I feel Wells tense next to me like he's gonna knock Ethan out flat. But I beat him to it. He doesn't even see it coming, probably because I've never had a penchant for violence before. But you just don't fuck with the people I love.

My fist connects with his cheekbone and nose, sending pain rippling up my forearm and into my elbow. But the look on Ethan's face is so worth it because he just looks so dumbfounded as he stands there with a bloody nose. God, I hope I hit him hard enough to give him a black eye. I wonder how he'll explain that one to his friends back home?

"Cunt." He spits at my feet, narrowly missing my new cowgirl boots.

"And you're done." Wells shoves him in the direction of where all the cars are parked. "Say another word and I will put you in the fuckin' hospital."

Ethan wipes the blood from his nose, turns on his heel, and storms away. The adrenaline that has been coursing through my body for the last fifteen minutes has dissipated. I need some air.

Wells grabs my hand and starts to inspect the knuckles. He sighs and lets it drop. I guess I didn't break anything.

"River?" I turn to face her.

"Um, yeah?" She looks like she's biting back a smile.

"Let's go meet Betty."

"You sure?" She walks toward us.

"You don't have to, Poppy. If you want to go find Rhett—"

"I am not going to find Rhett right now. He needs to cool the fuck off, and so do I," I tell Wells. "I'll talk to him tonight. Right now, River and I are going to go meet Betty. You good handling the rest of this?" I ask him.

"Yeah, of course." He smiles at me, looking very proud. "Good hit, city slicker. Wouldn't have thought you had it in ya."

I just roll my eyes. "Thanks, I think?"

"Oh, it's a compliment."

With a wink, he's jogging back into the barn, hopefully to get the rest of those sweet dogs adopted by the end of the day. I take a deep breath and look over at River.

"Ready?"

She smiles, and it's warm and playful. I can see why — if there is something between her and Wells — he likes her.

"Lead the way."

—————————◆

"So…" River says as we sit on my living room floor. Betty has been let out of her crate, and she's lying in between both of us, chewing on her favorite toy. She hasn't let River touch her yet, but she's been slowly moving a little closer, inch by inch. It's just going to take time.

"Wanting an explanation about what happened at the barn?"

She laughs. "Yeah, my life is boring as hell. I could use some excitement."

"Ugh," I groan. "I moved here from San Francisco, which I'm sure you know. I'm guessing word travels fast in a town this small."

"You could say that." Her grin is all I need to know about how much the people in this town know about me. I could probably get my social security number from one of them if I asked.

"Well, I left Ethan there. I broke up with him, let me make that clear. We were done. But he thought I would be back. I think most of my *acquaintances* I made while living there thought I would be."

"Acquaintances?"

"Yeah. I wouldn't call any of them friends. We weren't that close. I move a lot. Like…a lot. So I tend not to put roots down in the form of friends because it just makes it harder to leave when I'm ready."

"But you're more than friends with Rhett, it seems…" She smirks.

"I was ready to stop moving all over. I kind of just want a place to call home." I sigh. "That's why I took this job. I thought it would be such a wild change from what I'm used to that it might be exactly what I needed."

"Turns out you were right."

I hum my agreement.

"I've never seen Rhett look at anyone the way he looks at you," she tells me. "And the scene he made in the bar that night?" River laughs. "Yeah, way out of character for him. He's smitten."

"He's an asshole."

She throws her head back, her raspy laugh getting Betty's attention.

"Never said he wasn't. He just seems to be less of one when it comes to you."

I take a page out of Rhett's book and just grunt because I really don't know what else to say. I'm really, really mad at him right now. And while I know I am going to have to face him later and hash this shit out, I don't really want to think about it right now.

"So…you and Wells?"

"Uh, no." Her eyebrows pull together, and she shakes her head. Betty moves a bit closer, sniffing River's hand that's lying on the wine-stained rug next to her. "No, we're just friends."

"Oh, I'm sorry. It just looked like something."

"No, I just kind of grew up here?" Her tone goes up at the end like she's asking herself a question. "I guess. I don't know. I was here throughout all of high school because my house just wasn't all that fun to be at. So Wells and I are like brother and sister. Same with Rhett and Dean."

I catch on quickly. "But not Hayes?"

"Not Hayes." Her cheeks blush, and she looks down, suddenly very interested in the stain. "Hayes and I…it's complicated."

"You don't have to tell me." I reach out and squeeze her arm. "But if I need to kick his ass for you, I think I proved I'm more than capable."

We both laugh.

"I may take you up on that." The laughter settles, and she sighs as her head drops back onto the couch behind her. "I don't know. Whatever it was, it ended badly. And I haven't been back here for a very long time. But I miss it. Seeing Wells and Rhett and the animals…felt like coming home."

"I get that. I've only been here for the summer, and this ranch already feels like my home. And Katherine and Clyde?"

"So cute, right?"

I groan. "So cute. Welcomed me into their house and hearts so quickly. I've never felt so loved."

"They have a way of doing that. They're such good people."

"You're coming to my birthday party tonight, right?"

"Eh." She cringes and shakes her head. "I don't think that's a good idea. It's a miracle I escaped Hayes at the event."

"He's out covering for Rhett," I tell her. "That's why he wasn't there. They needed someone to manage moving the rest of the cattle. But he will be there tonight. I think everyone will. Katherine has made this a huge event." I smile and roll my eyes.

River nods and stares down at Betty.

"You should come."

"I don't know, Poppy."

"Look, if this is going to be my home, I'm going to need friends, right? No more acquaintances. So come to my birthday party and hang out with me and see the people you've missed."

She looks like she's considering it, so I keep pushing forward.

"And fuck Hayes," I joke. "Just ignore him."

"That, I'm afraid, is impossible." She sighs.

I get that. Rhett is impossible to ignore, too. No matter where he is, I find him, and vice versa. I would never be able to be in the same space as him and ignore him.

"Come." I'm pretty much begging at this point, but I don't want her to miss out on things because of a man. Especially when it seems like this family is so important to her. "If he bugs you, come find me. I'll be your buffer."

"You'll be speakin' with Rhett." She raises an eyebrow.

"Yeah, but not the entire night. And if he continues to be an ass, I may be the one that needs a buffer."

"Okay, okay. I'll come."

"Good." I smile, feeling like I've started to make my first real friend in years. "Want to help me feed Betty? She'll open up to you much faster if you give her food."

"Sure." River laughs. "Just show me how you do it."

CHAPTER FORTY

Rhett

WELLS TEXTED me to let me know I was an idiot. Then I got a message from Hayes saying that he heard everything that happened and that I'm an asshole. And then Momma called to let me know I would still be attending Poppy's birthday no matter how far the stick up my ass has gone.

Always has had a way with words, my momma.

And it's not like I didn't intend to go. My kids are still in love with her, and, shit, so am I. I'm in love with her. It's no excuse, but that's why I reacted the way I did. I saw him walk in, go right for her, and the second he wrapped his arms around her, my vision went fuckin' red. When he insinuated she would be leavin', going back to the city with *him*…I lost my shit.

So now here I am, walkin' over to the main house where the party is takin' place. The kids ran me late, so I know everyone is probably angry as hell, thinking I've decided not to come. But when the kids decided last minute to make their own birthday cards for Poppy, I couldn't say no.

The sun is already set by the time we get over there, making the massive bonfire Pops and my brothers made stand out like a beacon. Jesus, you'd be able to see it from the damn road. My nerves are stirring in my stomach something awful because I know I'm about to face fucking trial with Poppy. And I know she isn't going to hold back. I wouldn't want her to, but damn, it's gonna be bad.

Joey and Wade run ahead once we get to the house, yellin' about who is going to find Poppy first. I hope it's either of them and not me. Maybe they can soften her up a bit. The music is blasting, and there are trucks backed up to the fire with people sitting on the beds as they talk and drink and eat.

Hayes sees me first and storms over.

"The fuck did you do?" His finger is pointed right at me.

I groan. "Don't start."

"Don't start?" His eyes go wide like he can't believe that just came out of my mouth. "If you fucked up the first good thing that's happened to you since your kids, I'm going to beat the shit out of you."

"Would you calm down?"

"You know what he called her?" Wells pops up out of fuckin' nowhere. "You know what she did?"

"What are you talkin' about?"

"Well, be gentle with her hand. It's gonna hurt for a while." Wells smirks. "She punched the hell out of him. Gave him a good nosebleed."

"She did what?" It's my turn for my eyes to go wide.

She *punched* him? Woman is a firecracker.

"And then I threatened to put him in the hospital because he called her a cunt." Wells looks angry now. I'm surprised he was able to control his anger enough to not lash out. It's not like him to stand down with shit like that. He loves a good fight. "And spit at her feet."

He better be on a goddamn plane with no intention of coming back because I will kill that little shit if I ever see him again.

"Weak," Hayes says. "No man worth his salt is gonna speak to a woman that way."

"Looked like he had soft hands." Wells grunts. "Refused to shake 'em."

"Where is she?" My voice comes out as a growl.

"Well, it seems she's made friends with River." Wells has his best shit-eatin' grin on as he looks over at Hayes.

Hayes looks pained but nods over to where Poppy and River are sittin' together, laughing and drinking on a truck bed. Her booted feet are swinging, and she's still wearin' my hat. A whoosh of breath leaves my lungs. She's still mine.

My fist clings to the gift bag filled with wildflowers and the present the kids and I picked out for her. I told them people normally put colored tissue paper in the bags for presents, but Joey was determined to fill it with flowers instead.

As I watch her, Wade finds her first, grabbing hold of her legs as she reaches down to lift him onto the truck bed in between her and River. Joey isn't far behind, and they all lean together to read the cards they made for her. I can hear her laughter from across the yard as she throws back her head, holding on to the top of the hat so that it doesn't fall off.

She's stunning.

I am awestruck by her. All the time. She knocks me on my ass...daily.

Just when I'm about to close the space between us, she looks up, like she can feel me. Our eyes meet, and it's like I can't breathe. She sucks the air right out of my lungs when her smile doesn't falter. Poppy doesn't look at me like she hates me, and I can't fucking move.

"You gonna fix this?" Hayes asks.

"He has to. I refuse to lose the help." Wells grins when I look over at him.

"You won't," Hayes tells him. "Because if he doesn't fix it, I'll swoop in to be the rebound. And once she's had me —"

"Finish that sentence, Hayes Black, and Momma will be cryin' over your grave this time next week." I give him a look, and he and Wells both just laugh and back up with their hands in front of their chests. Little shits.

"Alright. Wish me luck." My palms are sweating as I grip the gift bag, wiping the other on my jeans. Jesus, this woman makes me feel like a kid caught with my hand in the damn cookie jar.

"Get on your knees if she won't listen," Hayes adds.

"She'll listen," I hear Wells tell him as I start to walk toward her. "She might show him her right hook first. But she'll listen."

CHAPTER FORTY-ONE

Poppy

I WON'T PRETEND I'm not angry, but seeing Rhett walking across the yard with a literal bag full of flowers in his hand, looking nervous as hell, has eased it a bit. God, I love that man. Through the anger and the hurt, I love him. And if he's showed up tonight, that must mean there's still something here that we can work on.

"Still wearin' my hat" is the first thing he says when he walks up to me.

"Never did like doing what I was told."

"I was thinking about getting some of Katherine's famous cobbler," River says, looking back and forth between us. "Maybe the kids want some?"

They both scream and carry on, jumping off the truck bed to dance around in circles on the ground. I can't help but laugh as I watch them, my loud, happy family.

"I highly doubt either of you have had dinner yet," I tell them, effectively bringing down the mood. They both groan and roll their eyes.

"Poppy's right. Can you at least eat a few bites of something *before* stuffing your faces full of cobbler?" Rhett asks.

"How about we just go fill our plates with anything and everything we want?" River winks down at them, and I have a feeling she will not be enforcing the real food first rule. Oh well, worse things have happened than kids having dessert for dinner.

Rhett waits until they walk off before holding my present out with a straight arm. He looks ridiculous, just standing there all sheepish while holding a bag full of wildflowers. It's oddly endearing seeing him like this. I'm used to the Rhett who has nothing but grumpy quips to say. Not the Rhett that struggles to look me in my eyes.

"Joey was insistent that we fill it with flowers instead of tissue paper," he says as I start pulling them out and laying them on the truck bed next to me. He sits down and watches. "And I personally don't think you need what we got you."

I finally get to the present and pull out my very own cowgirl hat. It's a beautiful tan color, with a dark brown rope around it that instantly reminds me of the rope Rhett tied me up with.

"Mainly because I like seeing you in mine," he says as I run my fingers along the smooth felt.

"Even though you told me to take it off?" I can't resist — I had to get a jab in. And this conversation has to start somehow.

He sighs and takes my hurt hand in his own, running his thumbs over the knuckles. I hit Ethan really hard, and I've never punched anyone before, so I had no clue what I was doing. That led to poor form, which has resulted in bruised knuckles and a very sore wrist that seems to be a bit swollen.

"You punched him." He brings my knuckles to his lips, and my stomach does about a thousand somersaults.

"He deserved it."

"I'm sorry I wasn't there to do it myself."

"You were too busy not listening to a thing I had to say."

He sighs and tugs me closer to him, so close that I can smell my favorite cologne. I use a spritz of it every time I steal one of his shirts, wanting to sleep with the smell when I'm in my own bed.

"Poppy." His hands run up and down my forearms and then hold my hands. He finally looks me in the eye. "I fucked up. I saw him touch you, pull you close to him, and then heard him talk about takin' you back to the city…I saw red. I saw my ex standin' there, not you.

"Everything came rushin' back," he continues.

"How Leah left me and the kids for the city, how Dean has left us over and over again for the damn bottle, and how Addie left us for good."

I reach out and wipe a stray tear from his cheek. My heart hurts for him.

"I know," I whisper. "It triggered you."

"It felt like my heart was being ripped out of my chest." He clears his throat and rubs his sternum. "I'm so, so sorry, Poppy."

"I never expected him to show up. Literally never entered my mind. I broke up with him, firmly, when I left the city. But, like everyone in my life, he expected the least of me and assumed I wouldn't be able to stick something out for the long haul. Because I never have. But I want this, Rhett. I want us. I want this ranch and this family."

"I saw the possibility of you leavin', and I thought I should be the one to hurt you first so I don't end up looking like the idiot."

I laugh quietly. "Yeah, you sure saved yourself looking like an idiot, Rhett Black."

"I know, I know." He groans. "Poppy, you asked me if I wanted the same things as you. The babies, the house filled with loud love, the grey hair and rocking chairs...I do. I want it all. With you. Only you. I was worried that if I asked you to stay that I would be holding you back...that you would end up wanting a life bigger and more exciting than the one I can give you."

He takes a deep breath.

"But I want you to *stay*, Poppy. Forgive me, please. Stay with me. *Choose* to stay with me, and I will work my ass off every day to deserve you. I love you. I am so fuckin' in love with you, baby. Stay. Please."

I smile, tears threatening to spill over as I forget we're surrounded by people and climb onto his lap. Straddling him, I grab his face and force him to look at me. Because I need this to sink the fuck in.

"I choose you, cowboy." I kiss him. "Every time. I choose this life with you. I choose your kids. I choose your family. I choose this whole fucking ranch. I want it all, Rhett. I want everything you have to offer and nothing else. I love you."

His hands run up my back as he pulls me in as close as I physically can be, kissing me hard as our tongues dance together. My arms are wrapped tightly around his neck, and we just fit together. My grumpy cowboy.

Somewhere in the background, I become aware that people are clapping and shouting as we make out on this truck bed. So I pull away, laughing when I turn around and see everyone watching us. Normally, I think I would be embarrassed, but not with Rhett. I want him to claim me in front of all of these people.

Everyone should know that Rhett Black is officially mine — off-limits.

I look around at everyone here, smiling and clapping for us. Katherine and Clyde are standing off to the side,

Clyde's arm around Katherine's shoulders as they watch us with nothing but love on their faces. Wells is shaking his fist in the air, making stupid noises, while Hayes stands next to him, staring over at River and the kids like he's in pain just being near her.

"I'm going to need all the details about whatever happened with River and Hayes," I tell Rhett, turning my attention back to him.

"That, poppyseed, is something you'll have to get out of them. Because none of us know."

The kids come running over to us, their plates piled high with food. Surprisingly, I see things on there other than dessert. And out of the corner of my eye, I see Hayes making a beeline for River. She tries to walk away, but he corners her, leaning in to speak as close to her as he possibly can.

My hackles raise, and I want to go over and save her, be the buffer I promised I would be. But the kids are handing us their plates so they can climb up in the truck with us, and Rhett refuses to let me move. When the kids are settled with their plates on their laps, I try again, but Rhett captures me, holding me tightly to him with his arms wrapped around my waist.

"You're not goin' anywhere," he tells me, his voice all deep and raspy. "I've got you, and I don't intend to let you go."

There was a time earlier this summer when I would've fought back. I couldn't stand the guy when I first met him, and fighting back just to get him riled up was my favorite pastime. But now I can't stand being away from him. I crave his nearness and his touch, the way he smiles at me, the way he holds me.

It feels good to have a home — a home with Rhett, Jolene, and Wade.

"I *told* you that you should marry our daddy," Jolene says through a mouthful of cobbler.

Rhett sighs.

"What have I said about speaking with your mouth full?"

"We aren't married, baby girl." I smile over at her. "We just love each other very much."

"Well, whenever you do get married," she says, very confident in her stance on this, "I want to be the flower girl."

"What do boys do?" Wade asks. "I want to do somethin'!"

"You'd have the important job of holdin' on to the rings for us, bud," Rhett tells him.

Wade nods like this is an acceptable answer to him.

Before I can say anything to Rhett about any of this, the music dies out, and everyone starts singing "Happy Birthday." Rhett helps me turn around and climb down to watch Katherine carry out the most beautiful cake I have ever seen. Clearly handmade, but made with so much love I'm afraid my heart is going to explode.

Rhett stands behind me, his arms wrapped around my torso as we sway back and forth.

The cake is covered in candles and Katherine's handwriting in icing that says, *Happy Birthday, Poppy*. The singing ends, and she holds it out toward me.

"Make a wish, poppyseed." Rhett kisses my hair and releases me enough to lean forward and blow out the candles.

"What did you wish for?" Wade asks, his little voice filled with curiosity.

"Something happy," I tell him vaguely, smiling over my shoulder at Rhett.

Because what *exactly* I wished for…well, that's a secret. Everyone knows if you say your birthday wish out loud, it won't come true. And when I look over at River and Hayes, arguing quietly next to the buffet of food, I know I've made the right choice.

I have everything I could ever want. Why not spread the love?

EPILOGUE

Poppy

Three months later…

"YOU'RE SURE this is what you want to do?" Katherine asks as she stares at all of us standing on her front porch.

I'm in a long-sleeved white sundress and the cowgirl boots I bought this past summer. My hair is freshly dyed Rhett's favorite peachy pink, I'm wearing the cowgirl hat they got me for my birthday, and I'm freezing. Who knew Montana was so cold in the fall? Not me.

"It was her idea." Rhett shrugs and laughs. "Who am I to turn down the woman I love?"

"But we need to stop and get flowers," Jolene says. "I need to have some flowers to throw around when they're done!"

"I've already got the rings!" Wade roars, showing

Katherine the little box that holds two gold bands. Mine has pretty floral etching in it, and Rhett's is just plain yellow gold. We've had them for a while now, having gone to pick them out only a month after my birthday.

I'm tired of not wearing them.

"Alright, let me go get my shoes on!" Katherine starts digging through piles of shoes in the entryway until she finds her boots. "Clyde!" she shouts into the house. "Your son is getting married!"

"Which one?" he calls out.

She groans. "Who do you think? Rhett, you old man. I'm going to be the witness. We'll be back."

Clyde walks out into the hallway, grinning ear to ear. He takes me in a hug so violent I'm worried my ribs are going to crack.

"So happy to have you officially in the family," he says, his voice cracking on the words. He sets me down and then firmly shakes his son's hand, pulling him in for a rough hug at the end. "Proud of you, son," he whispers. "Always have been, always will be."

"Okay, okay," I say, taking a couple of steps back, fighting the tears. "We have to go, or I'm going to start crying, and I would like to last through the ceremony."

Clyde sniffs and smiles, letting Rhett go but giving him a firm pat on the shoulder. They lock eyes for a moment, something unspoken being passed between them, and then we're off. The kids run toward the truck, Katherine scooting in the back with them and buckling them in. As always, Rhett lifts me into the front seat, kissing me hard before running around the front.

"This is so exciting!" Jolene sings from the back. Her little feet are kicking like crazy as she bounces up and down. Both of them look so freaking cute in their fancy clothes that I want to squeeze the absolute life out of them. Wade is even in little suspenders that make him look far too old for my liking.

"Ready?" Rhett asks as he slides in.

"Giddyup, cowboy."

The town courthouse has a green dome on top. It's made of copper, Rhett tells me, and was once new and shiny. But over the years, it's turned a muted green color because the town doesn't have the money to constantly clean it. But it oddly works with the rest of the old brick building.

We walk inside, getting the marriage license signed and notarized before being led down to the room they use for weddings. I guess we just got lucky that there's a judge here today. I didn't really think about that before suggesting that today be the day.

But it all works out. Katherine and the kids stand off to the side, Wade clenching that little box with all his concentration and Jolene holding her little bouquet of flowers. My family.

Rhett stands in front of me, his nicest jeans and button up shirt on. He's wearing his cowboy hat, and I'm so full of love for this man I think I might burst. Never in a million years did I see myself here, getting married to a rancher I met only a few months ago, but the heart wants what it wants.

"Have you both prepared vows, or would you like us to use the standard ones?" the judge asks.

"We did—"

"We prepared our own." Rhett's voice interrupts my own...shockingly. Because I did not write my own vows. We literally decided to do this about two hours ago. Where the hell did he get the time?"

"Okay, then," I drawl. "I guess we wrote our own?" I look at him, my eyes wide and confused.

Rhett just winks at me.

"When I first met you, Poppy Sharpe, you infuriated me."

Off to a good start.

"There were so many things about you I didn't like. You talked back. You had my brothers wrapped around your finger. And my kids were smitten with you."

"What's smitten mean?" I hear Wade whisper.

"Means you liked her a lot," Katherine answers.

"Oh," he says.

"But," Rhett says, trying not to laugh, "I came to

realize that all of these things that drove me crazy were actually the things that made me love you. You challenged me. You loved my family. And you accepted and loved my kids."

I squeeze his hands and try to blink away the tears. I didn't expect this from my grumpy cowboy.

"I promised you on your birthday that I would work every day to deserve you. And I want to promise that again now. Poppy, I promise that I will wake up every day loving you, caring for you, and working to earn every bit of happiness you give me. I will go to bed loving you and wake up choosing you."

"That was beautiful," I whisper, not trusting my voice. I'm a mess, tears sliding down my cheeks so quickly I can't stop them.

"Poppy?" The officiant turns to me, and I nod, realizing I'm going to have to wing this.

"You can read the standard vows if you want, poppyseed. I know I threw this on ya," Rhett teases.

I narrow my eyes at him, making him laugh, and clear my throat of the ache that always accompanies crying. This is why I never brought up doing our own vows because I knew I'd be an absolute mess.

"Rhett, even though you're the grumpiest cowboy I've ever met, I've fallen in love with you. From the way you treat your mother to the way you love your children. And even though you drive me absolutely insane sometimes, I wouldn't have you any other way. I love you, and I promise to keep on loving you every day. I promise to choose you and this life we make together for the rest of our lives."

I turn toward Jolene and Wade.

"I love you both as well, and I promise to be the best I can be for both of you. I promise to give you all the love I have to give every day. I'm not just marrying your daddy; I'm marrying this family. Thank you for giving me a safe place to land."

"Thank you," Rhett mouths when I turn back toward him.

The officiant says some stuff, but honestly, I'm too ready to kiss my husband that I miss everything. I barely register Wade coming over with the rings, Rhett putting mine on and then me putting his on him.

But what I do register is Rhett scooping me up in his arms as he kisses me. He kisses me so hard that his hat pushes mine off. Katherine grabs it, and then Jolene is throwing her flowers in the air in front of us. The kids squeal and cheer, picking up the flowers and throwing them over and over again as Rhett and I get lost in each other.

"We're married," he says, pulling back to look at me. I get the warm and fuzzies all over again when I see the joy in his honey-brown eyes. "Thank you for marrying me."

"You're welcome."

He throws his head back in laughter, and it's contagious, making my own bubble up out of my chest.

"God, I love you so much."

"I love you, too, cowboy."

THE END

Want a sneak peek of Hayes & River? Keep reading to see how their story starts.
You can pre-order *Untamed* now!

SNEAK PEEK OF UNTAMED

"SURPRISED TO SEE YOU HERE, DARLIN'."

My entire body freezes. I should've known there would be no way I could escape this moment. Ever since I moved back to town, I've been avoiding him like the plague. But since his brother basically forced me to come back to their ranch in order to adopt one of their rescue dogs, I knew he'd find me like a damn heat-seeking missile.

I've successfully avoided him all day, sneaking around the barn with all the rescues while he worked and then hanging out with his brother Rhett's girlfriend all afternoon. But when Poppy begged me to come to her birthday bonfire, I knew it was a bad idea. I tried to get out of it, knowing that Hayes would find me, but she looked stressed about her fight with Rhett and so hopeful that I would come keep her company.

I caved.

But I refuse to look in his direction, instead focusing on the grape salad that's in front of me. I was trying to fill my plate with the sweet marshmallow and brown sugar stuff before he decided to drop in. And now I'm just...frozen. My arm is outstretched over the table filled with food, and my fingers dig hard into the plate I'm holding.

"I'm sure you are." My voice finally comes, but it's unsure and quiet. I haven't spoken to him in over a decade. Not since we fought. Not since I told him I never wanted to see him again. "And don't call me darlin'," I add. Because that's what he always called me, even when we were kids. And my heart can't take that kind of ache.

"Right?" he asks. "Because I'm pretty sure the last thing you said to me was that you never wanted to see my narcissistic, hypocritical, smug-ass face again." He hums like he's thinking hard about it. "Did I miss anything?"

"Ugly."

"Ouch."

I shrug. "Leave me alone, Hayes. I'm only here because your brother practically dragged me."

"Which one?"

I sigh. He knows which one. Rhett is too grumpy to speak to anyone but Poppy. Dean is in rehab — at least, that's the last I heard. And Wells is the one I'm still friendly with. He knows it was Wells, and the fact that he's just trying to get more of my attention is annoying as hell.

"Wells." My voice comes out cold and hostile. Good. I want him to leave me alone.

"Why would Wells drag you here?"

"God, can't you ever do as you're fucking told? Just respect people's boundaries and walk the fuck away?" My temper spills over, and I instantly regret it because when I finally turn to face him, I'm assaulted with memories of us. It's like a car crash I can't look away from. His dirty-blond hair is hanging out from under his black cowboy hat, and his blue eyes look ornery as hell in this firelight. That little smirk on his lips makes me want to kick him in the shins.

"River—" he starts.

"I've been wanting a dog." I decide just to tell him as quickly as I can. The faster I quell his curiosity, the faster he'll leave me alone. "And Wells wouldn't help me rescue one until I came out to the ranch to see him and your momma and pops. Then Poppy begged me to come out to her birthday party, and I caved. Because she's sweet and new here, and I'd like to be her friend. I didn't come here for you, or to talk to you, so just leave. Me. Alone."

"You're gettin' a dog?"

"Yes," I grit out. "And I'll have to come out here every day for a while. Because Betty has to get used to me before I can take her home. I'll try to make sure I'm only here while you're out working so that we won't cross paths."

He scoffs and crosses his arms over his broad chest. I try really, really hard not to get distracted by his fore-arms. They were always the object of my fixation. From years of playing guitar and working on the ranch, they're strong and tan, and my fucking god, I'm distracted.

"Don't put yourself out on my account."

"What? What do you want from me, Hayes? I wasn't kidding when I said I never wanted to see you again. Why would you think that had changed?"

"Why'd you move back here after college, then?"

"Oh, my god."

I laugh, but I don't find it funny. I'm angry. I'm so incredibly angry at him that I toss my plate down on the table, losing a few grapes in the process, and lean in toward him. We're surrounded by people talking, music playing, and the bonfire crackling, but I still don't want to draw attention to us. I'm sure his parents know something happened because I was here every damn day of my childhood, running around this ranch, trying to keep up with the boys and then playing with Addie in the evenings.

I don't want them to know what happened. The embarrassment would end me.

"I came home because my momma needed me to help her with bills." I couldn't say no. No matter how shitty of a mother she was to me, I couldn't let her starve or lose the house. And it's not like my sister, Jane, could just leave her job and husband in New York. "Coming back to Cane Creek had nothing to do with you, Hayes. I dreaded it. I loved my life in Bozeman, and I knew if I came back here, I would run into you no matter how hard I tried to avoid it. But Momma needed me, and I couldn't say no."

I can feel the tightness in my throat that always comes with crying. But I will not break down here, not in front of him. He is no longer my rock or my best friend. He is no longer my confidant.

"I'm sorry, River." The sympathy leaks into his features, and it makes me want to scream. I didn't want this. I don't need whatever he wants to give me. "That has to be tough. I know you had big dreams."

My big dreams involved him and only him. He was all I wanted. Anything else was just a happy bonus. I would've stayed here and lived a peaceful life on the ranch. I love this place. It wouldn't have been a hardship to live this life with him.

"I don't need your sympathy, Hayes. I just need you to leave me alone. Please."

"I'm sorry that bein' around me is such a hardship for you, darlin'."

I can feel my entire body flush red with anger. And I'm really about to give him a piece of my mind when he opens his stupid mouth again, crushing me all over again.

"Most women don't find it so difficult."

I close my eyes for a moment, smiling even though I feel anything but happy in this moment. But I need to take a breath because he's winding me up on purpose, and I refuse to feed into this game he's playing. I lick my lips and then look back up at him.

"Alright, Hayes. We get it." I pick my plate up and add one more scoop of grapes. "You're a fuckboy, and you have women throwing themselves all over you. So go get one of them to give you the attention you crave. I am not going to be that person for you anymore."

I pop a grape in my mouth and then walk away, leaving him to stand there alone like the asshole he is. Looking over to where Poppy was when I left her, I see her cuddled up to Rhett while his kids eat their plates of food I helped them pile high with sweets. I am definitely not interrupting that little moment.

So instead, I go over to Wells. He greets me with his warm signature smile and wraps an arm around my shoulders, shaking me lightly as he hugs me.

"Hayes botherin' you?"

I laugh, chewing on another grape, the marshmallow cream and brown sugar making my teeth hurt in the best way.

"When isn't he bothering me?"

I refuse to look back at him, but Wells doesn't. Wells looks over my shoulder, grinning, and then fucking winks at him. These men. They've always known how to pester the shit out of each other, pushing buttons until they're fighting with their fists in the back-yard. Clyde had to break them up once when Hayes pissed Rhett off so badly he left Hayes with a broken nose and a bloody lip.

"Don't start," I tell him, a warning tone to my voice.

"What?" He looks down at me, smiling wide with ornery eyes.

"Don't 'what' me, Wells Black. I know how y'all work. Leave it be."

He kisses the side of my head, and I fight the urge to look at Hayes for the rest of the night.

Untamed is now available for pre-order from your favorite online retailer.

ABOUT IVY JACKSON

Ivy Jackson is a lover of quiet small towns, nights where you can see all the stars, and the smell of hay being cut (even though it sends her allergies into overdrive). She grew up in a tiny village along the Ohio River where there was nothing better to do than ride four wheelers, go cow tippin', and get into far too much trouble at Friday night football games.

You can follow her on her socials:

Instagram & TikTok - @author.ivyjackson
Facebook Group - Ivy Jackson's Small Town Smuts

Or visit her website to get all the info, as well as signed copies and swag:

www.ivyjackson.com

ACKNOWLEDGMENTS

Hi all! Thank you so much for reading Burned. I hope you enjoyed it as much as I enjoyed writing it.

First, I want to touch on the subject of Cystic Fibrosis. I've always wanted to write a book where I got to talk about the disease that ultimately took my aunt. I got so many great years with her, and I am so thankful for each and every day we spent together. CF is a rare disease, one we are still studying and learning about daily. Some will need double lung transplants, like my aunt did, and others will just need treatments throughout their lives.

Many will struggle to breathe normally, to gain weight, and with coughing and repeated lung infections. Life expectancy with this disease is constantly changing thanks to the hard work of scientists and doctors. My aunt was told she wouldn't make it to thirteen. When she surpassed that, they told her eighteen. After that, it was thirty, and then forty. A week before her 40th birthday, we got the call. I remember my mom waking me up at two in the morning, telling me that my aunt was going in for surgery at Cleveland Clinic.

I was young, about eleven, I think, but I knew it was a big deal. I knew she wouldn't need to do her treatments anymore – no more breathing in those medications or struggling to make it up the stairs. It was an amazing miracle to watch. Over the years she traveled, started her own business, and gave speeches all over. She even met the family who tragically lost their daughter so that my aunt could receive two healthy lungs.

A few years ago, right before the pandemic hit, we lost her. The anti-rejection medication she had been taking religiously for her transplant ended up giving her stomach cancer. Her last months were brutal, and I've never seen someone in so much pain. But she was ready to go, and she felt as though she had served her purpose – teaching and helping others for as long as she was alive.

She was my biggest supporter and would be thrilled I was able to do something I loved. This book is dedicated entirely to her and all the love she gave me.

Now, let me wipe my eyes and take a deep breath, because we have more people to thank!

To my alpha/beta readers, thank you so much for reading this as I wrote it and for all of your feedback.

Reading your comments every day – especially during the spicy scenes – was the best. You guys had me cackling.

To Sandra, my editor, thank you for going through this at lightning speed. Fast as fuck, boi. You devoured it and knowing that you loved it so much has made my heart happy.

Tori, my proofreader and formatter, thank you for giving my book baby some extra proofing love to make sure she is as good as she can be. And thank you for bringing the pages to life with your formatting.

I had two covers done for this book. The model cover was done by Cady at Cruel Ink Editing and Design, and let me tell you, that woman knows what she's doing. And Jillian at Blue Moon? Lord, have mercy. I saw that discreet pre-made and snatched it SO fast. I knew it had to be mine. And I can't wait to see what both of you make for the future titles in this series!

Readers, thank you for taking the chance on Burned. I poured my heart and soul into this sucker. These characters were speaking to me for ages before I could put pen to paper, so when it was finally time, it was just an outpouring of love as I typed. I genuinely hope you enjoyed the love between Poppy, Rhett, and his two beautiful kids.

Now, who's ready for Hayes?

Milton Keynes UK
Ingram Content Group UK Ltd.
UKHW011844071223
433887UK00004B/206